Jake wasn't just a beach bum who lived only to play...

"Taste this, Ariel," Jake said, holding out a spoon dripping with chocolate, unaware of the swell of hope inside her. He was just going to feed her again, as he'd been doing since the day she arrived, a perfectly innocent gesture.

But this time it would mean more. Ariel gripped his wrist, pulled the spoon to her lips and slowly licked it, holding his gaze, her heart pounding, her pulse racing. *What am I doing?*

Jake's eyes flared.

"Mmm," she said, telling him she wanted more... much, much more. So much more that it would mean tearing down the sheet that acted as a wall between their beds.

"Ariel," he whispered, then leaned in to kiss her. In the background she heard the phone ring, but this was one time she *wasn't* going to answer.

Dear Reader,

This is a story about how love smoothes people's rough edges, just as the waves polish stones on the beach. And Ariel Adams clearly needs some smoothing—even her name sounds sharp. And Jake Renner, for all his laid-back-beach-bum facade, needs Ariel to show him he's outgrown looking ahead only as far as the next wave.

I share Ariel's tendency to be ruled by plans and arrangements. I share her trouble with balancing work and fun, being able to say yes to something spontaneous. Writing about Ariel's endless lists gave me a good laugh at myself.

And of course I adore Jake—he reminds me of my own husband, who loves water sports, too, and has a keen sense of fun. I love the way Jake nurtures Ariel with food and gives her permission to relax and enjoy life.

I hope you love Ariel and Jake as much as I do.

Best,

Dawn Atkins

P.S. I'd love to hear what you think of this book. Please write me at dawnatkins@cox.net. You can learn about my upcoming books at my Web site, www.dawnatkins.com.

Books by Dawn Atkins

HARLEQUIN TEMPTATION
871—THE COWBOY FLING
895—LIPSTICK ON HIS COLLAR

HARLEQUIN BLAZE
93—FRIENDLY PERSUASION

HARLEQUIN DUETS
77—ANCHOR THAT MAN!
91—WEDDING FOR ONE
  TATTOO FOR TWO

ROOM...BUT NOT BORED!
Dawn Atkins

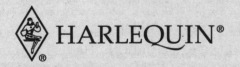

HARLEQUIN®

TORONTO • NEW YORK • LONDON
AMSTERDAM • PARIS • SYDNEY • HAMBURG
STOCKHOLM • ATHENS • TOKYO • MILAN • MADRID
PRAGUE • WARSAW • BUDAPEST • AUCKLAND

To David, for making love so easy

ISBN 0-373-69145-9

ROOM...BUT NOT BORED!

Copyright © 2003 by Daphne Atkeson.

This edition published by arrangement with Harlequin Books S.A.

® and TM are trademarks of the publisher. Trademarks indicated with
® are registered in the United States Patent and Trademark Office, the
Canadian Trade Marks Office and in other countries.

Visit us at www.eHarlequin.com

Printed in U.S.A.

1

IN HEELS AND A BUSINESS SUIT, with two monstrous suit-cases in her sweaty grip and her computer bag slung over her shoulder, Ariel Adams stood on the stone stairs that led down to the beach cottage she'd just acquired. She blinked against the silver flash of California sun on gentle waves and wondered what she'd done to deserve this hell.

Okay, so most people would consider the rippling ocean and white-sand beach where a man juggled drift-wood for a rapt retriever and seagulls dipped and cried, to be picturesque and enticing—perfect for sunset strolls, refreshing swims and building sand castles. But Ariel Adams was not most people.

To her, the beach was too...beachy. A giant cat box with a shifty surface tough to walk on and a fishy smell. The beach meant grit and mildew and sea salt that scoured, stained and bleached everything.

No, Ariel did not like the beach. And now she had to live there. Her left eyelid twitched from exhaustion. Ter-minally jet-lagged after the flight from London, all she wanted was to sleep for a week. But she couldn't afford that luxury. She had to figure out how to start her solo consulting business two years earlier than she'd planned. She sagged against the rusted guardrail, demoralized, until she repeated her mother's motto in her head: *Keep on keeping on.*

Job one of keeping on was to cross this beach without ruining the high-dollar silk panty hose she'd bought in honor of her new life in London—the life her partner Trudy had thrown out the window. The twenty-seventh-floor office window of their client Paul Foster to be precise. That high up, the windows didn't even open.

Paul and I are in love, Trudy had breathed, airy as a romance heroine, as if that were enough to explain how a perfectly sensible woman—Ariel's mentor in this very male business—had turned into a doe-eyed fool.

Ariel had reasoned with her. *Give it six months. Be certain your feelings will last.* But no. Two days of harangues hadn't cleared one iota of the sentimental glaze from Trudy's face. Paul was taking a world tour of his holdings before he retired and Trudy was going with him. *When love comes, you accept it, wherever it may lead,* Trudy had said in that feminine trill she'd adopted. Had her hormones gone wonky? Had she been hypnotized? Slipped a cog? What?

This was not the plan. And planning was king at Business Advantage, Trudy's company, into which she'd invited Ariel six months ago. They'd met when Trudy had been hired to assist with a business consolidation and Ariel had been working in-house for one of the merging companies. Trudy had been so impressed by Ariel's talent that when Paul Foster retained Business Advantage to go to London to help the Foster Corporation make a strategic shift, Trudy had asked Ariel to become her partner in the firm—to help with the project and beyond.

That had suited Ariel just fine. Her plan had been to work with Trudy for two years—or until she felt ready to be on her own. But that plan was all gone. Trashed by Trudy. For love.

Foster had gone weird, too. Falling in love had made him decide to sell the company and *live life to the fullest*. Double blech. In his defense, he'd also had a cancer scare— a misdiagnosis, as it turned out—that had made him reassess his values. Ariel was all for businessmen reassessing their values—but to *advance* their businesses, not abandon them.

She'd so looked forward to the London experience. It was the opportunity of a lifetime to be instrumental in a highly visible corporate evolution, and meant a huge leg up for her business reputation. It would give her cachet, to be elegant about it. Not to mention international contacts. And London itself had been amazing.

But now, only three weeks into the adventure, she'd had to catch a flight back to L.A. to start her business with just a name, Trudy's file of stale leads and her own bravado.

Before Ariel left, Trudy had given her what was left of Business Advantage, which wasn't much, since Trudy and she had finished with their U.S. clients before the London move.

And now Ariel was on her own. With a sigh, she descended the sand-scrubbed steps to the beach house in Playa Linda, where she would live until she was financially able to move somewhere more appropriate.

Trudy had felt so guilty about abandoning Ariel, she'd practically given her the cottage, asking a ridiculous price, payable over time, that Ariel couldn't afford to pass up. Even though living there would be like camping, the property was a prize piece of real estate. Lots of people thought beach living was nirvana.

And at least she had a home. Before the move, she'd given up her tidy apartment, contoured precisely to her habits, and put her belongings in storage along with their office equipment.

Five steps down, Ariel's heel skidded on grit and she tilted to the side, banging her elbow on the rail.

A guy with a surfboard caught her arm from behind. "You okay, ma'am?"

Ma'am? She was only twenty-nine, darn it, no *ma'am*. She could be this guy's date, not his mother. It was how she was dressed, she was certain. Her dark tailored suit, high-necked blouse and efficiently bunned hair made her seem as out-of-place as a Victorian matron in a strip club. "I'm fine," she snapped, and the guy trotted on without a backward glance.

Ariel finished the steps and started across the sand, stepping carefully so as not to grind sand into her delicate stockings. The cottage was nestled into a low hill, with a basement garage accessible from the narrow street. If Ariel'd had the garage door opener, she could have entered that way and avoided the beach altogether, but some things couldn't be helped.

With each wobbly step, her sleep-deprived mind churned out more bad thoughts. What if she didn't get clients right away? She was good, she knew. She'd saved an entire division during the consolidation she and Trudy had worked on together, and the clients she'd handled for the six months she'd been part of Business Advantage had been very happy. The baby clothes boutique had doubled its profits, thanks to her, and her diversification plan had saved a computer parts manufacturer from a painful downsizing.

Handling the clients was no problem. What stopped her heart was the idea of selling herself to them in the first place. That had been Trudy's specialty. Trudy knew promotion. She knew how to coax and cajole. In that regard, Ariel was lost at sea. A critical liability when starting a business from scratch. What if she starved? No way. She was a survivor and a worker, just like her mother. Ariel's father had died when she was just three, but her mother hadn't moped a minute. She'd gotten two jobs—at a laundry and a diner—and always made ends meet.

It sounded grim, but her mother was never discouraged. Adams women kept on keeping on. Ariel had spent many happy hours playing dolls under the diner tables. The waitresses talked to her in their rough, practical way—barking at her to get out from underfoot during the busy times, joining her to act out a quick Barbie and Ken date during the lulls. And to this day, the smell of laundry soap cheered her.

She would survive, all right, Ariel thought, marching forward in the thick sand. If worse came to worst, she'd get a job at a temp service or take some contract work—rare, of course—with another business planner. This was just a setback. Sweat poured down her sides under her expensive suit. That meant a dry cleaning bill. She tried to think cool thoughts as she lunged forward, lugging the bags that wouldn't roll on the soft sand. Almost there, almost there.

Then, she was there—Trudy's beach getaway, now

her very own. Small, faded and shabby, it looked as if a good wind could topple it. She'd remembered it as more attractive that one weekend she'd spent with Trudy here laying out the plans for their partnership. Her spirits flagged for a second.

Quaint and cozy...with rustic charm. That's how she would describe it in the real estate ad she intended to place as soon as she was flush enough to move out. *You'll look back on this and laugh,* she told herself, closing her eyes for a quick visualization....

She and her husband walking among the roses in front of their ranch-style home in Thousand Oaks. His warm voice in her ear: *Remember when you were a desperate newbie in a ramshackle hut cold-calling clients to afford food?*

She would tip her face up to his—of course he'd be much taller—gaze into his dark eyes and give a tinkling laugh. Maybe not tinkling. Trudy's laugh had tinkled. A gentle laugh then.

Look at you now, her dear husband would continue. *You've hired an associate so you have more time to spend with me, your adoring husband. Shall we swim?*

Then they would walk arm-in-arm to their Olympic-sized pool with the dramatic black surface and bricked rim and swim slow laps, looking into each other's eyes. Oh, and their golden retriever would run along the pool's edge as they swam....

Much better. Ariel sighed and opened her eyes, rejuvenated by her vision of the glorious future she'd push herself to, no matter what. Now to get started. Except she hadn't slept in thirty-six hours and she was so tired....

Keep moving, she told herself fiercely. *You snooze, you lose.* She marched up the stairs to the porch, her fingers burning from holding the suitcases, which clunked up each step. Sweaty and breathing heavily, she extracted Trudy's key from her purse and put it in the lock, only to have the door yanked away from her from the inside. She stumbled two steps forward and into a man, connecting with his warm, solid, *naked* chest.

He gripped her arms, steadying her, holding on a few seconds longer than necessary while he studied her. His fingers were strong and reassuring, his eyes a Brad Pitt smoky blue.

"Well, hel-lo," he said, propping her back onto her heels.

Unbalanced by the surprise—and the man—she'd only managed, "Hello," before a black-and-white bear of a dog rushed past them from inside the cottage. On its heels was a young boy wearing a green baseball cap, who paused to slap the man on his muscular shoulder and yell, "You're it!" before racing down the stairs and across the beach after the dog.

"Time out!" the man shouted to him, then lowered his gaze to Ariel's. "Sorry. Jake Renner." He lifted her limp hand and helped her shake his, his eyes full of laughter at her shock.

"Ariel Adams," she said faintly.

"Can I help you?" He was a little taller than she was and blond, with a deep tan on a muscular body that was pretty much on full display except for baggy Hawaiian-print swim trunks. He was way too relaxed for someone who'd been caught squatting in Trudy's empty beach house.

"Is this Trudy Walters's place?" Maybe she'd arrived at the wrong ramshackle cottage. She could only hope.

Something trilled sharply. For a second, in her exhaustion, she feared it was her brain warning it was about to blow. But it was just her cell phone, good for only two more days before service expired.

Jake Renner leaned against the doorjamb and watched her fumble for her phone.

"What?" she said irritably into it before she'd actually activated it. Pushing the button, she said, "Hello?"

"Ariel?" The faint voice belonged to her love-crazed ex-partner.

"Thank God, Trudy. I'm at the beach house, and, you won't believe this, but—"

"There's a man there. I know," Trudy said. "I didn't get the chance to tell you. I hired him before we left for London to paint and do some fix-up so I could sell the cottage."

Ariel glanced at Jake—his hair was beautifully sun-streaked—then turned to the side to make the conversation more private. "I wish you'd said something."

"I'm saying it now. And there's one more thing...." Uh-oh. "He might be living there. As part of the deal, I told him he could stay until he finishes."

"You told him he could live here?" Her voice squeaked. She shot Jake a wan smile.

"It's good to have someone keep an eye on things. This was killing two birds with one stone."

"You should have warned me."

"I was a little distracted, I guess. And you took off so fast.... Jake's a nice guy—completely trustworthy. He's done work for my neighbor, watched her kids while she did errands. Very sweet. I talked to him several times."

"But he's going to live here?" Ariel whispered through gritted teeth. "With me?" Again, she tried to smile at Jake.

"There are two bedrooms, Ariel. And he's not going to attack you or anything...unless you want that." Then her voice went low. "If I'd had the time, let me tell you...wowsa."

Wowsa? So un-Trudy-like. "Why are you telling me this?" she said, exasperated, hoping the cell phone hadn't leaked Trudy's words to her eavesdropper.

"Love is all around, Ariel. Stop and smell the roses."

Smell the roses? All Ariel could smell were dead fish and seaweed...and maybe a faint coconut scent coming off Jake Renner's gleaming body. "I'll get back to you on that," she said, her saccharine smile going sour. Her partner—who had yanked herself up by the straps of her own Aerosoles and, by the way, had once declared relationships speed bumps on the road to success—was now spouting Zen bumper stickers from her outpost in the Twilight Zone.

"I mean it," Trudy insisted. "Rethink your life. I've started doing watercolors again."

Ariel held her tongue.

"I'm sure you can work something out with Jake. He's very easygoing."

Ariel shot a glance at him. *Easygoing and hard-bodied.* He exuded that lazily confident air that most women went for. She got a little internal zing herself. Biology was undeniable, she guessed, no matter how inconvenient.

"Look at it this way," Trudy continued. "If you don't like the paint colors or tile I chose, you can change them—on my dime. If you want, add a few things while he's available."

"I can't afford anything more. I don't want anything more. I...oh, hell, this is just too much to think about."

"You'll do great, Ariel. Soliciting clients is not that hard. Your work speaks for itself."

Not if she couldn't speak for her work.

"Start with my leads, use my software and call me if you need a consult. If I'm anywhere I can be reached by phone, of course." She gave that laugh again. More a trill than a tinkle, now that Ariel thought about it. "Seriously. You have everything you need to be successful."

Everything except clients. "I appreciate your faith in me," Ariel said. "I'll talk to you soon."

"Bye-ee."

Bye-ee? What had the twit on the other end of the line done with levelheaded Trudy? Was she wrapped in duct tape in a trunk somewhere? Ariel clicked off, thrust the phone back in her purse, and looked up at the nearly naked man wearing a bemused expression.

"So I guess you're the house painter," she said, trying to smile.

He bowed. "And the framer and the carpenter and the plasterer and, possibly, the electrician, judging from the shorts we're getting in the bathroom."

"Shorts in the bathroom?" she repeated weakly. Her already fuzzy brain throbbed with this new quandary. She didn't deal well with change. Someone had definitely moved her cheese. "I need to sit down," she said, bending to grab her suitcase handles, intending to head inside.

Jake took the bags from her, hefting them as though they weighed nothing, and held the door. She moved inside, sand grinding in her shoes, anxiety burning in her stomach. She caught more of Jake's scent as she passed—warm sunshine, sweet musk and coconut—pleasant in a beachy kind of way.

She looked around the tiny living room and her heart sank. There wasn't even a place to sit. Drop cloths covered what few pieces of furniture fit in the small space. Pieces of Sheetrock were propped against a canvas-covered lump—the sofa. Boards lay on the floor along with boxes of nails, tools, masking tape and a few cans of paint. More drop cloths covered two side chairs and the cocktail table.

There were two fancy bicycles leaning on one wall—one disassembled—and a colorful, battered surfboard braced against the half wall that led to the kitchen.

Jake set down her bags, shoved some of the sofa's canvas away, and motioned gallantly for her to sit in the space he'd cleared. She dropped there with an unladylike plunk.

"Better?" he said.

"A little."

Jake lowered himself onto a drop-cloth–covered chair very close to her, the muscles of his legs and chest rolling with his movement. How she managed to fixate on his body at a time like this was beyond her. It must be raw exhaustion. Like a hypnosis subject transfixed by a shiny object, she couldn't take her eyes off him. *You're getting sleepier and sleepier...warmer and warmer...more and more aroused...*

"Things are a little confusing," she said, trying to clear her head. "Trudy sold me this house while we were in London and now..."

"And now I'm fixing it up for you. No problemo." He had the bluest eyes and an expressive mouth—very broad, like it spent most of its time smiling.

"Yes, problemo," she corrected. "I have to live here, you see. And work here. And—"

"Not to worry. I'm a great roommate."

"I'm sure you are, but, I don't really want a roommate." *Or a construction site.* Jake obviously wasn't one of those craftsmen who prided themselves on working neatly. Supplies were scattered from one end of the room to the other. God knows what the rest of the house looked like.

"I don't either, but I'm flexible." He shrugged. "You can have the master bedroom, since it's your house."

She stared at him. "As I just said, I would prefer the place to myself."

He looked at her, blinked, smiled.

"I'm a business consultant," she explained. It was difficult work that requires concentration, quiet and order and—at the minimum—a room for an office. She surveyed the living room and it looked the way her life felt—confused and chaotic. Despair welled up. She rested her elbows on her knees and held her head in her hands.

"You're freaked right now," Jake said softly. "Give it a few days and see how it works out."

She lifted her head and stared at him.

He grinned. "What, you want to kick me out today? Make me sleep on the beach?"

"I'm sure you have family or friends you can stay with."

He just looked at her with those smoky blue eyes. She knew silence was a negotiating tool meant to put the opponent on the defensive, get him to blurt a concession, and she felt herself succumbing, maybe because Jake was disconcertingly handsome and so...naked. And his eyes seemed to see more than she intended to reveal. "You just get into town?" he asked gently.

"Yes. I just flew in from London."

"And, boy, are your arms tired."

"Funny." Not.

"Just kidding. You look beat. Why don't you get out of that monkey suit and get some rest? When you're feeling better we can talk this all out, calm and easy."

She stifled the urge to point out that they had talked it out. She would stay; he would go. She'd give him a bit to realize she was serious. She didn't want to come across too harshly. It wasn't his fault Trudy had double-booked them.

"Come on and I'll show you your bedroom." He took her by the elbow and helped her to her feet. She usually disliked men she'd barely met presuming to touch her, even casually, but this felt okay—friendly and helpful, not pushy—and he let go of her as soon as she was upright.

She walked beside him to the short, narrow hall that led to two bedrooms and a bath, her elbow still warm from his fingers.

"I'll move into this room," Jake said, indicating the

guest room. What had been a tidy room, accented by lacy pillows and silk flowers when she'd stayed with Trudy, was packed with equipment—oxygen tanks and rubber scuba suits, big duffels, some with fins sticking out, a pole with rope hanging off it, possibly the boom of a sailboat, two more surfboards, one of which had a sail, and a stationary bike.

How could anybody even find the bed, let alone sleep in it?

Even worse, the room was missing most of one wall. Through the ragged edge of Sheetrock she could see straight into the second bedroom and the rumpled bed where Jake must sleep.

"There's no wall!" she exclaimed, turning to him.

"Wood rot from a ceiling leak, so I had to knock it out."

"How can we...you...? I mean...we can't sleep like this!" They might as well be in the same room.

"I don't snore, I swear," he said, then read her face. "We'll put a sheet up if you want. And, relax, I won't bother you—no sleepwalking or...whatever."

She knew what he meant by *whatever* and was a tad miffed he'd said it so fast. She was reasonably attractive, but he'd written her off like the dude with the surfboard who'd called her *ma'am*. She put her hair in a bun because it was efficient and it revealed her neck—one of her better features. "The sheet will do for tonight," she said firmly, ignoring the wound to her femininity. "And you can make other living arrangements tomorrow."

"Check out your room," he said, ducking below the top edge of the torn wall and stepping over the baseboard. He offered his hand. She ignored it—she could climb into a room on her own, thank you—and joined him. The master bedroom was only a couple feet larger than the guest room, and held more Jake debris—personal items in cheerful disarray—swim trunks on the floor, T-shirts in a corner, a guitar and a weight bench. He'd really made himself at home in the three weeks he'd been here.

Jake reached past her to pick a pillow off the floor, which he tossed onto the rumpled bed. "Sheets are pretty fresh—washed yesterday—but I'll change them if you want."

"I'm sure they're fine," she said.

"It's a great mattress. Try it out." He motioned at it.

She flashed on the activities that would call for him to put the mattress through its paces and tensed. "I'll take your word for it." No way was she lying on a bed looking up at a mostly naked Jake.

He bent beside her and grabbed a T-shirt and some shorts, his thigh muscles flexing, his trunks tight over his butt. Wow. Jake might act lazy, but there was nothing lazy about his body. Not an ounce of fat hid the muscles of his legs, arms and back, and his abdomen was corrugated, thanks, no doubt, to the weight bench. The fleeting image of Jake pumping iron turned Ariel's insides to jelly.

Jake stood. She dragged her eyes away, but too late. He caught her staring and grinned. "I'll clear out my gear later so you can catch some zs. Take your clothes off, though. You'll sleep better."

"I'll be fine," she said.

He seemed to be disrobing her all on his own, so she crossed her arms over her chest.

He smiled. *You got me,* his eyes cheerfully conceded.

That friendly X-ray stare made up for Jake's earlier dismissal. Superficial of her maybe, but as a woman she felt better.

"How about I make you a protein and banana smoothie?" he said. "You need potassium. Flying zaps your salts."

"Thanks, anyway. I'm really fine. Sleep will help."

"When you get up then." Jake left the room, taking up the entire doorway as he went. She realized he'd shrugged off the eviction like she hadn't said a thing. She'd rectify that later—be polite, but firm. Exhaustion and the undercurrent of attraction had weakened her usual resolve. She'd take a power nap and bounce back.

Making sure the bedroom door was locked, she took off her jacket, blouse and skirt—*the monkey suit* Jake had called it—and slipped her bra off under her slip, which she'd sleep in.

Removing her shoes, she carefully peeled down her silk stockings, pleased the sand hadn't damaged them. She folded them and placed them on the bureau. Then she collapsed onto the bed and shut her eyes. It felt so good to lie down. Everything would seem better after a nap.

Jake's coconut smell rose to her nose from the pillow—pleasant, if too intimate. It was thoughtful of Jake to suggest sleep.

She was just drifting off when she heard a series of bangs, clunks and rattles from the kitchen, which was so close in the tiny house it might as well have been in her room. Then came the horrific roar of a blender. Jake making a smoothie, no doubt.

After that, someone pounded on the front door. She heard a kid's eager voice, a dog's bark and the scrabble of nails on the wooden floor. God. Her new home was close quarters for two people, especially when one of them was as noisy, popular and, she was forced to admit, attractive as Jake Renner. So much for peace. So much for sleep.

Jake better find a place to stay right away, or she'd find him one herself.

2

JAKE GAVE RICKIE a couple of boards and some paint and promised to help him with the tree house tomorrow. Rickie had haunted the beach house from the moment Jake arrived three weeks ago. He was lonely and his parents were divorcing, so Jake had played catch with him a couple times, then introduced himself to Rickie's mother, so she'd know he was okay. Then he'd met the sitter—a definite dating prospect, which enhanced things considerably.

He couldn't break away now, though. He had the bike to fix for Barry and he wanted to be around when his new roommate got up. He turned his CD player down a little, in deference to the sleeping woman, though he thought he'd heard her moving around.

Jumpy. The way she'd barreled into him at the door showed she was wired for action. If she hadn't been so tired, she'd have had him packed and out on his ass right now. Despite her jet-lagged befuddlement, her knotted hair, business suit and erect posture spoke volumes about her personality. Gung-ho, no nonsense, maximally serious.

He wasn't moving out, he already knew that. He'd given up his closet of a basement apartment and he liked having room for all his equipment in one place and living where he was working. Besides, he couldn't afford rent if he wanted the scratch he needed to fund his sister Penny's trip.

He'd have to get Ariel comfortable living with him—make her life as smooth as the gearing on Barry's Guerciotti, which he was working on right now—so she'd forget all about him leaving.

He adjusted the triple-gear unit, then spun the pedals. Much better. He liked getting his hands on equipment. That was one thing he'd learned from his father, Admiral Shipshape—how to handle machinery. It made up a little for the commands and the regulations and the misery when he was growing up.

His father better not be as hard on Penny as he'd been on him. Penny claimed not, but she was too sweet to fight back.

That made Jake remember that she was planning to check out the beach house this weekend. Not a good idea with his landlord on-site. Having a teen guest—even one as smart and sweet as Pen—would definitely annoy Ariel Adams. He put down the bike and grabbed the phone to postpone the visit a couple weeks.

"Renner residence, Jake here." His father. Damn. He hated talking to the man, hated that air of disappointment—thick as the slabs of beef his dad loved to grill in the back yard—that permeated every conversation.

"Hello, sir."

"Jake Junior, how are you?"

"Fine, sir. Penny there?"

"Yes, she is." Pause. Stern silence. "You haven't been to the house in two months."

"I've been busy. Charters and a house-painting job..." He let his words trail off.

"You owe it to your mother to present yourself from time to time."

For inspection. Shoes shined, tie straight. His dad was Navy to his bones. "I'll come out in a week or two."

"Saturday, the fifteenth? I'll let her know."

"That depends...." But the last thing he needed was another argument with his dad. "All right. The fifteenth."

The admiral was silent on the other end. He had something else on his mind or he would have gone for Penny. These conversations were as awkward for him as they were for Jake. "Made any progress, son?" he finally said. That was Admiral Renner code for settling down—having a real job, a wife, becoming a man with responsibilities, debts, burdens.

"Every day is progress, sir," he said with a sigh. He'd be damned if he'd do anything in life the way his dad had done it.

Silence. Then his father said tightly, "I'll get your sister."

Why did Jake's heart thud after these exchanges? He was almost thirty years old. It was the shame in his father's voice. His only son was a footloose bum he couldn't brag about with the other officers, whose kids were in the Academy or the diplomatic corps or were lawyers or computer whizzes. He felt the shame heat his face. Ridiculous. What did he care what his narrow-minded father thought? Unlike his father, Jake enjoyed life. Enjoyment was not a duty, so Admiral Renner didn't make room for it.

And as far as being footloose, that was something he'd learned as a kid, thanks to his father's transfers from naval base to naval base—Virginia to Florida to California. Jake had learned how to let go when he needed to. Now, when things got weird or dull or troublesome, it was easy to just leave.

As a kid, it had hurt, being forced away from things he loved—the swim team, girlfriends, great buds, even teachers who'd inspired him. But he got used to it and it taught him to be flexible, open to new things that were just as worthwhile.

Moving around had been tough, but that was only the launching pad for his struggles with his by-the-book father. Jake had never met a rule he liked, and he made sure his father knew it.

"Hey, Jake," Penny chirped.

"Hey there, Squirrel, how are you?"

"Good. I got second place in the swim meet."

"Terrific. Did the Admiral stop picking on you about your grades?" It wasn't until he'd left home that Jake realized that Penny might be paying the price for his rebellion. His parents were overprotective and kept her close to home, under watch.

"He wasn't picking on me. He was concerned about me, that's all. Parents do that. It's a duty."

"There's more to school than grades, Pen. Don't let him browbeat you."

"Chill, would you? I want good grades, too. For college."

"There's plenty of time for college. You have to live life." As soon as she graduated high school, he was making sure she got to spend a year in Europe. That was what she wanted, though she'd stopped talking about it. He'd seen the flyer on her desk when he was home at

Thanksgiving—*Study Abroad. See Europe and earn college credit*. He'd asked her about it and she'd sounded so jazzed until she read him the costs. Then her enthusiasm faded. *Too much money*. She didn't have to say it.

That was when he decided he would make it happen. He'd pay her way, arrange everything, including running interference with the old man. Jake would not let Penny suffer for his sins. As soon as she had her high school diploma, he'd break her out of the brig his parents kept her in.

"So, I can't wait for this weekend," Penny said. "You can teach us to surf—I'm bringing Sheila. She wants to sailboard."

"Um, that's kind of why I called," he said, hating to disappoint her. She asked for so little from him—or anyone. "We'll have to postpone the trip for a couple weeks."

"Postpone it? Why?"

"The living situation has changed. It turns out the owner sold the cottage and now I've got a landlord living here."

"So, we'll bring sleeping bags and crash on the floor."

"Not yet. She's a little touchy right now."

"She? Your landlord's a woman?"

"Yeah."

"She single?"

"Why does that matter?"

"So turn on the Jake charm already."

"I'll be lucky if she doesn't kick me out on my ass."

"Does she have eyes? Ears? A libido?"

"Libido? That is not a word you should even understand, let alone use."

"I'm sixteen, Jake. I'm a woman. With womanly needs."

"That's enough of that." The whole idea creeped him out. "You take it slow. You have your whole life to get involved in…that stuff…." He felt himself flush. Penny needed a solid guy who would look out for her, worship the ground she walked on, and only when she was mature enough to get serious.

"Yeah, yeah, whatever," she said. "You sure I can't come?"

"Sorry."

"I guess Mom and I will rent movies or something."

"Go out with friends. Don't let them trap you at home."

"They don't lock me in a tower. If you're so worried about me, talk your landlord into letting me stay. What's her name?"

"Ariel."

"That's pretty. Is she? Pretty, I mean."

"She's all right." Compactly built, with everything in the right place from what he could see through the business suit. For a moment, he thought of sleeping with her. Bad idea if he wanted to live here through the summer and maybe beyond.

Sleeping with a roommate was a mistake he'd learned from Charlotte. She'd agreed they'd keep it light, just enjoy each other, but then she wanted to know where he was every minute, pouted if he wasn't home for dinner, acted like a wife, for God's sake. Then he'd hurt her feelings. He'd hated that. Why did women think they could change him? Why did they even want to? He was who he was and that ought to be enough.

"So, why not...see what happens?" Penny said.

"We are not having this conversation, Pen."

"Okay. I just wish you'd find someone special so you'd stop hassling me."

"I'm just looking out for you."

"Then get me invited to the beach house."

"I will. As soon as I'm sure I'm staying."

"If she's a woman, you'll be staying."

He wasn't sure how to take that and did not like his sister even hinting about his love life. "Do something fun this weekend," he commanded, then hung up, his roommate jumping into his mind. She'd be hot in bed, he'd bet—active, motivated, goal-oriented. Useful traits in the sack. Hmm.

Nope. He needed Ariel as a roommate, not a play-mate.

A PUFF OF DAMP AIR blew Ariel awake. Had she left the window of her London flat open to the drizzle? She opened her eyes just as a wet, black blob snorted at her. Focusing one eye, she made out an animal muzzle and realized it was attached to the dog that had burst out of the house when she'd first arrived. Pleased that he'd awakened her, the dog pranced a couple of steps, then shook itself mightily, spraying water and sand every-where.

The reality of Ariel's situation came back to her like a belly flop in the pool of her stomach. Gone was the charming London flat she'd shared with Trudy, re-placed by a cramped beach house jammed with water sports junk and construction debris. She picked up the sound of rock-and-roll playing in the front of the house and a woman's teasing laugh, followed by Jake's voice.

The dog, poised near her face, gave a desperate whine—*get up and play*. When Ariel didn't move, he loped to the more interesting side of the house.

She felt gritty all over—her skin, her hair, her eyes. It wasn't her exhausted imagination, she learned when she found sand on the sheets and pressed into the undersides of her arms.

The fading light told her it was dusk. Woozy and not a bit rested, she looked at her travel alarm, which she'd taken from her bag when Jake's banging around the cottage woke her for the third time, and saw that she'd only napped for an hour.

She looked at the giant hole in the wall between her room and where Jake would sleep. Judging from the lush sound of that woman's voice, Jake might have company tonight. She'd like to tell him no—the last thing she wanted to hear were erotic moans and headboard banging—but she wasn't sure she wanted to bring up sex with him in any regard. She'd only have to put up with his nocturnal guests for one night, maybe two, until Jake moved out.

Ariel brushed off the grit, climbed out of bed and went to the bureau mirror to see if she looked as bad as she felt. Oh, yeah. Her hair had come loose from her bun, her mascara formed exhausted semicircles under her eyes and she had the indents of sand pebbles all along her left cheek.

She felt something soft under her feet and found her silk stockings in a tangled wad. Clusters of holes and long runs decorated the delicate silk. She'd protected them from sand damage only to have that monstrous dog nose them off her bureau and ruin them. She didn't even have the energy to work up a fit of temper at the dog. At least she had a second pair in her suitcase.

"Jake, don't," the woman called in a tone that meant *don't stop.* Feminine wiles and coy flirtation. Blech. Ariel didn't play games. If she wanted to sleep with a man, which she did from time to time, she showed him with a deep kiss, or responded favorably to his caress. Or she just plain suggested it. Why get silly about something so basic and human?

Of course, lately, with Business Advantage consuming her attention, there hadn't been much time for sex. Which was probably why she kept getting snagged by the sight of Jake's body. Once her career was in order, she would open herself to a relationship. The timing would be perfect.

Now, she'd unpack, then write up business and personal to-do lists. Lists would put a fence around her whirlwind of worries. She had to make progress before she went to bed for the night or she'd never fall asleep.

She glanced around the jam-packed room. She'd have to pry Jake away from the Playmate of the Day and get him to clear out his junk before she could even unpack. Then she'd pin him down on the time frame on the cottage renovation.

That meant looking decent enough to appear in the living room. Ariel ran a brush through her hair, changed into a linen short set and slipped into the bathroom to repair her makeup. She wasn't primping exactly. She just didn't want to look as bedraggled as she felt. At the last minute, she dabbed perfume on her wrists and neck.

Peeking around the hall corner, she saw that Jake and his friend, who wore a bikini that consisted of three bandage-sized triangles held together by dental floss, were dancing swing style to some nouveau jitterbug. The dog jumped up now and then as if to cut in—to dance with Jake, not the woman, who laughed in that lush way that meant business, sexually.

Jake smiled, but there was distance in his expression. *Don't get too close.* She wondered fleetingly what it would take to get past Jake Renner's affable sexuality to what made him tick.

Not that that was any of her concern. The dancing made her smile, though, and set her thoughts wandering. She'd needed an aerobic exercise in college and selected ballroom dance since she'd be learning a skill and getting exercise at the same time. The grace and freedom of it had enchanted her. She'd met Grayson in that class and they'd begun their affair. She missed dancing. How long had it been since she'd moved to music, alone or with a partner? Once the business was stable she would have fun, too, she told herself. All in good time. And according to plan. Planning gave you freedom.

Jake caught sight of Ariel and stopped dancing. "Sleeping Beauty awakes," he said. "Heather, meet my landlord, Ariel Adams. Ariel, this is Heather."

"Hi," Heather said. Her expression was direct—*are you after him?*

No, thanks, she tried to communicate with her eyes. "Nice to meet you, Heather."

"You get some rest?" Jake asked her.

"Some." Except for the blender and the visiting kid and the giggling girl and the music and the snorting dog. But there was no point getting technical. "Sorry to interrupt," she continued, "but I was hoping you would clear your things out of my room...?"

"I guess I should go," Heather said to Jake. "See you later tonight?" she asked, establishing ownership, presumably for Ariel's benefit. "For the volleyball game at Ollie's?"

"If I'm up for it," he said, his tone clearly saying *Don't push*.

Poor Heather. She probably hadn't figured out this guy was as elusive as he was handsome.

"We'll have fun. I promise."

"You don't need me to have fun," he said.

A tiny frown appeared between the woman's sharply plucked brows, and she looked from Ariel to Jake, assessing the danger of them getting together. In the end, she sighed, picked up a sarong and a beach bag from a drop-cloth–draped chair, said, "Ciao," and left. Jake watched her go, admiring her casually—like someone appreciating a work of art, knowing there was a museum's worth beyond it.

The dog watched Heather leave, then honed in on Jake, ready for action. When Jake made no move to follow the girl, the dog plopped onto its substantial belly, spread-legged, scattering sand.

"Is this your dog?" Ariel asked, praying it wasn't. The last thing she wanted was to be snuffled awake again by a sandy-pawed canine. Even one with eyes as big and brown as a bear's.

"Lucky? Nah, his owners live down the beach, but he hangs with me a lot. We're buds, aren't we, Luck Man?"

The dog looked up at him with pure worship on his doggie mug. *Sure are, boss.*

"Time to head home, pal," Jake said, "before your owners start worrying." He held the door for Lucky, who seemed to droop, like a kid called home for supper, and slowly walked out the door, his back end swaying regretfully.

Ariel couldn't help smiling at the sight.

Jake caught the look. "Great dog, huh?"

"He sheds a lot of sand."

"Be glad he didn't bring in another starfish. Hid one under the bed once. Talk about stink."

Great.

"So, I bet you're hungry," Jake said.

"Starving," she blurted. Her stomach rumbled in agreement. The last thing she'd had was a sad Salisbury steak on the plane.

"Good. I was just about to fix some *huevos whateveros.*"

"*Huevos* what?"

"Eggs with whatever I find in the refrigerator. Topped with salsa—I make my own."

"I don't want to put you out," she said. She should get unpacked first, but eating would give her the boost she'd need to look over Trudy's contact tracking software and gear up for making calls tomorrow.

"So I throw in a couple extra eggs. Easy." He started for the kitchen. "We're roommates, right?" he said over his shoulder.

Not for long, she wanted to say, but she'd give it a rest until they'd eaten. She could hardly expect Jake to drag that weight bench out of her room on an empty stomach.

She headed into the kitchen to help.

3

"WHAT CAN I DO?" Ariel said when she reached the kitchen.

"Just keep me company," Jake said. He opened the refrigerator and reached inside, demonstrating what a marvel of biological engineering his body was. Smoothly swelling muscles fanned out, tightened and released in delightful synchronicity as he shifted things around. And his skin was a golden brown....

Stop. What was she doing? Her travel-fogged brain kept honing in on Jake's anatomy. She should be worrying about the "whatever was in the refrigerator." If Jake was like most guys, it would be leftover Chinese, ketchup and maybe wilted lettuce.

She was relieved when he stood with an armload of fresh items—an avocado, some mushrooms, Muenster cheese and a plastic-wrapped container of what looked like fresh spinach.

"Are you sure I can't do anything?" she asked. *To keep from ogling you?*

"Not a thing," he said. The way he snapped on the gas stove, deftly whacked off a hunk of butter and flipped it onto a serious omelet pan seemed to indicate he knew his way around a kitchen—or at least an egg dish.

The kitchen was small—no, cozy, she corrected, thinking like a real estate agent. The counter space was modest, but charming—tiny blue-and-white tiles with decent grout. The sink, however, was battered and rust-stained and the faucet appeared corroded. She'd have to replace it. Kitchens and bathrooms were big selling features, she knew, and a good place to spend renovation dollars. The stove was an older model, but clean and it seemed to work.

The wallpaper was outdated, but high shelves held decorative plates with ocean themes, attractive driftwood pieces, and several plants—curly bamboo and an orchid—that gave the room character and life.

"I can at least set the table," she said, going to the cupboard beside him, where she assumed the plates were. She found flower vases, mixing bowls and sports bottles instead.

"Up there," Jake raised his chin at the cupboard directly above him, his hands busy cutting mushrooms.

"Excuse me," she said, reaching past him.

"Take your time," he said, not moving an inch. She felt his eyes on her, sensed his lazy grin, and prickled from the abrupt intimacy of it all. Snatching two plates, even though they didn't match, she decided to wait until Jake left the counter to get the water glasses from the higher shelf.

The silverware was in the first drawer she opened, thank goodness. Unwilling to hunt for napkins, probably in the drawer at Jake's groin, she ripped two paper towels from the under-cupboard hanging roll, then moved to the table, which held more Jake accoutrements—a bike repair manual, a set of wrenches and a stack of magazines named for S sports: *Sail, Scuba, Surf.*

"So, you seem to do a lot of water things," she said to make conversation while she set the table.

"Why else live at the beach? Being in water feels good."

Pool water, maybe, which was clear and clean, not mucky like the ocean and full of creepy weeds and mysterious creatures you couldn't see. Plus, saltwater burned her eyes.

Finished setting the table, she watched Jake efficiently chop a hunk of red onion into tiny squares that he sprinkled into the bubbling butter. Great hands.

Ariel forced herself to look away. Her gaze snagged on the kitchen linoleum. Bleached, scarred and cracked, it should be replaced. She hoped that was part of Jake's job. If not, she'd have to pay for it herself.

Now was a good time to find out what Trudy had asked him to do. She'd be gentle, not her usual blunt self. The man was cooking for her, after all. "I guess the construction company you work for gives you a lot of free time for your sports?"

Jake gave a short laugh. "Construction company?" He glanced at her as he picked up an avocado. Cupping it, he deftly coaxed it out of its hull with such easy grace she found it hard to swallow. "I work for myself."

"So, how, um, did you get into construction?"

"I'm not really *into* it," he said, fanning the slices in a gourmet-worthy display onto the cutting board. "I have buddies in the business." He began cubing the Muenster.

He'd learned construction from *buddies*? Drinking buddies, no doubt, who swapped construction feats of derring-do over pitchers of margs. The guy was a beach bum, pure and simple. A charming bum, but still a bum. Maybe Trudy's good sense had run amok long before she headed for London.

"So Trudy says you worked on her neighbor's place?" she asked, wanting some credentials.

"Yeah. It was fun. And then Trudy offered me this gig."

Gig? This was a *gig?* "So, you're not a builder, per se?"

"Nah. I teach scuba, sailing, surfing, repair bikes, this and that."

At least he had other income—he'd be able to afford rent *when he moved out.* "So, tell me what Trudy's asked you to do."

"This and that," he said, snapping eggs one-handed and lightning-quick into a bowl.

"Specify, please."

"Okay. Let's see…patch the roof…repair the wall between the bedrooms…deal with the electrical, replace the wallpaper in the living room and kitchen…paint inside and out…replace the kitchen linoleum with tile…" He looked up, considering. "That's it, I think."

"That's a lot," she said, grateful that Trudy had arranged to have so much done, but worried about living through the chaos of a messy worker. On the other hand, if she cancelled some of the work, when would she be able to afford it? "And how long do you expect it to take?"

"Two-three months. Depends."

"Depends on what?" What time he got up in the morning? Whether he needed to consult a manual? "That seems too long."

"You can't rush quality," he said, dumping the egg mixture into the omelet pan, pausing to deliver a wicked smile.

"Oh, yes, you can. I would think a month would be plenty. Let's aim for that. Speed is crucial since this will be my office, too, until I can afford to lease space."

"You won't get in my way," Jake said, sprinkling cheese on the omelet.

"But you'll get in mine," she said as gently as she could. "I'll try to meet clients in their offices—more convenient for them—but I'm sure I'll need to see a few people here, and I'll need peace and order for that. The second bedroom will be my office, but until you move out, the living room will have to do. That means the painting stuff must be organized."

"The sunporch would make a great office," Jake said, pointing a spatula in the direction of the door out back.

Through the window in the door, she could see tattered window screens, plastic patio furniture, another surfboard and lots of sand. "Hardly. I'll have business equipment—a computer, a printer, a fax machine. Wind and sand would ruin them. Not to mention how easy it would be to break in."

Jake jerked the pan so that the food-packed omelet neatly folded in half, and brought it to the table. "I can put up some Plexiglas and a solid door. The awning gives nice shade. Most people would kill for an office overlooking the ocean." He cut the steaming egg dish in two and slid one side deftly onto her plate, the other onto his, then sat across from her.

"But I can't incur additional expenses."

"Don't worry about the money. It'll work out."

"Money never works out without careful attention...." She was momentarily distracted by the omelet, which smelled so heavenly her stomach convulsed with joyful anticipation. "Anyway, I'd like you to finish the living room first. The electrical seems critical, as well. I'd prefer you do the noisy things when I'm not working—early mornings and early evenings—or at least coordinate with my schedule. When you're ready to start on the kitchen, I can plan for takeout meals."

"I'll handle the food," Jake said. "If you like my cooking, of course." He plopped a dollop of fragrant salsa—finely chopped tomatoes, onions and fresh cilantro—onto her portion of the omelet. "Give it a try," he said, pushing the plate closer.

She wanted to finish her plan first, but to satisfy him, she took a bite.

Oh. Wow. The buttery, cheesy eggs melted on her tongue. The mushrooms were a sweet musk, the onions tangy pearls of flavor, the salsa a spicy tomato garden. "This is *sooo* good," she said, barely pausing to swallow before taking another bite.

"I'm glad you like it." Their eyes locked and Ariel felt an alarming sizzle that made her stop chewing. Jake took in her face, then strayed to her chest in an involuntary carnal appraisal. He lifted his eyes to hers, looking pleased with what he'd seen. "Any dietary restrictions? Particular foods you like or dislike?" he asked, making it sound like he was asking after her sexual preferences.

"I like, um, everything." That sounded bad.

"I could resurface the wood floors, too, you know," he murmured, equally suggestively. "If I had enough time..."

He seemed to be trying to seduce her...with smooth omelets and gleaming wood floors. And it was working. Freshly surfaced floors would really make the place attractive to buyers....

Stop it. Jake was flirting with her, bribing her. "I can't afford the floors," she said, deliberately breaking the gaze.

Jake shrugged. *We'll see,* he seemed to be saying.

Ariel went after the omelet again.

Jake chuckled and she looked up, still chewing. "I like it that you're not afraid to enjoy food. I hate when women nibble and pretend not to be hungry."

"I'm not much on pretense," she said, swallowing her last bite. Jake still had half of his omelet.

"No, you get right to the point, all right," he said. "Like I know you want me to move out of here right away."

"I think that would be best," she said, putting down her fork with reluctance, glancing again at all the eggs Jake wasn't eating. She should have savored hers more.... "I've got a lot to handle and this place is too small for two people *and* a construction zone." She felt guilty ogling his omelet while she was talking about booting him onto the beach.

"Here," he said, cutting her a bite of his eggs and holding it out—an intimate gesture that he made seem perfectly natural.

"No, no. I'm fine." She shook her head. "I had plenty."

He moved the fork closer, tempting her.

She took the bite quickly, avoiding eye contact, feeling

shaky inside. Then the fabulous taste overcame her. "Mmm," she said. "This is amazing."

"People love my mixed grill, too. I stuff the meat with chorizo—do you eat meat?"

"Yes."

"Good. My enchiladas aren't bad, either."

"I can imagine," she said, loving the sound of that. She'd have to get an aerobic exercise plan immediately if she was going to eat any more of Jake's cooking...which she wouldn't be for any more than two days. At the most.

"And I make great coffee." He was hitting her where she was vulnerable, which, right now, was her stomach. "And I'm good company," he continued, leaning forward, very companionable, very warm.... She had the odd feeling he was tempted to kiss her. And, worse, she kind of liked the idea. She licked her lips, which made Jake take in a little breath before he continued speaking. "How do you feel about...?"

Kissing? Love it. Live for it. She felt herself sway toward him, transfixed by his great lips and teasing smile.

"Poker," he finished.

Poker? Was *poker* code for what she thought they were talking about?

"Yeah. I like to have people over for all-night games."

"All night?"

"Yeah. Five-card draw. There's an ante limit."

The daze cleared abruptly. What was wrong with her? Jake was talking about poker, not *poker*. She was obviously feeling overwhelmed by all the changes and the work she faced and was using this physical attraction as an escape valve. Talk about self-defeating. She had to focus on her goal, not on kissing or *poker* and any of its double meanings.

"So, you've only been here three weeks and you've got friends hanging out for poker and enchiladas?"

"I know people in Playa Linda, and I've lived up and down the coast. The marina where I work a lot is close. And I make friends pretty easy."

Friends like Heather, no doubt. Friends she didn't want sleeping over.

"I'm sure you're good company and you're a great cook, Jake, but the problem still stands."

He spoke in a John Wayne drawl, "This town ain't big enough for the both of us, Pilgrim. That what you mean?"

"Exactly."

"Do I make you uncomfortable? Is that it?" he asked, his blue eyes digging in.

There was no point in fibbing. "Yes, actually, you do."

"I don't mean to. You don't have to worry. I don't believe in fooling around with roommates."

"Excuse me?" She felt her cheeks go red.

"It's nothing personal. It just gets too complicated."

"Oh, it does?" she said. For some reason, she was wounded that he'd said that so easily—as if she weren't even a temptation. Her inner wild child purred to life—out of sheer stubbornness and exhaustion-induced recklessness.

"Somebody always wants to turn it into something it isn't," Jake added.

"And I'm guessing that somebody's never you."

Jake shrugged. "Living together triggers nesting instincts for women, I guess, and they start bringing in twigs and bits of twine and dryer fuzz."

"So you think any woman who lived with you would try to trap you into something permanent?" What an arrogant...

He grinned. "Good point. Not every woman, but why risk it? A good roommate is like gold."

"I doubt you'd find me a good roommate. I like spic-and-span orderliness and absolute peace and quiet. And classical music."

"Classical's good. And don't be so down on yourself."

"I'm not down on myself. I'm trying to tell you—" She stopped, realizing he was teasing her.

"It's all right, Ariel. I'll find a place to crash for a while—maybe stay on a friend's boat. Can I keep my gear here though?"

"Your gear? If you can fit it all in the guest room closet, I guess." She remembered the sailboard and surfboards and the weight bench. No way would that fit in one small closet. She sighed. "Take a couple of days," she said, "and find a place for you *and* your stuff."

"Great." He sounded relieved. Too relieved. She would stay on his case until he was out. Fully out. Surfboards and all.

"Thanks for the food," she said, picking up her scraped-clean plate and his. She'd do the dishes as a thank you.

"I'll clean up when I get back from volleyball," Jake said. "Why don't you come with? I'm heading out in a couple hours."

"No thanks." Playing was the last thing on her mind.

"How about if you clear your things out of my room, while I do the dishes?"

Before he could respond, there was a thump at the door. Jake went to answer it. Lucky bounded in with *did ya miss me?* all over his doggie face.

"So you smelled the omelet, huh, pal?" he said to the big dog. "She ate your share." He stuck a thumb at Ariel, but Lucky didn't take his eyes from Jake. "Okay, okay. I'll scramble you something."

"I thought table scraps were bad for dogs."

"But eggs make his coat shiny," Jake said, ruffling Lucky's fur. "He likes my cooking, don't you, Bucko?"

Ariel did the few dishes while Jake cooked eggs for Lucky. When he'd finished, he slipped the pan into her soapy water.

"So you'll empty the room now?" she reminded him.

"Yes, ma'am," he said with a fake salute. "Let's roll, Luck Man. We have our orders."

Lucky swiped his buttery mug with a long pink tongue, then galloped eagerly after Jake. Ariel's gaze snagged on Jake's terrific butt, the muscles flexing and releasing with grace and power. With a jolt she realized she was letting soapy water drip onto her feet. *Stay on task,* she told herself. At least she'd gotten Jake to move out of her room. Next would be the cottage.

But when she peeked into her bedroom ten minutes later, the only change was a pile of vintage Hawaiian shirts on the bed—tossed there from the open closet, which still held a variety of footwear like hiking boots, cycling and athletic shoes and Velcro-strapped sandals, as well as another surfboard.

Jake stood at the bureau flipping through a magazine

while he did one-handed wrist curls with a substantial hand weight, Lucky at his feet, looking up at him. *What's next, boss?*

"How's the moving going?" she asked. "Can I help?"

"Fine." He smiled at her, his biceps swelling with a slow curl, his triceps rippling with its release.

Her objection died on her tongue at the sight of all that power on casual display. She averted her gaze and noticed a photo on the bureau. Four people were pictured—a stern man in a uniform, a pretty woman with a pageboy cut, a young girl and a teen boy—Jake with shoulder-length hair, dark baggy clothes and a sullen expression that was the opposite of the carefree, wise-ass look she'd seen so far.

"So, this is your family?" she asked.

Jake stopped lifting weights and looked over her shoulder. "Yep. Ten years ago or so. I was nineteen, I think."

"You don't look too happy."

"I wasn't." He studied the photo. "My father and I fought—he was career Navy and I was as far from ship-shape as I could get myself."

"That must have been rough."

"Everybody rebels," he said, but she could tell there was more he wasn't saying.

"So you moved a lot? Being in the military?"

"Some."

Standing close to him, she was aware of how broad and sturdy he was and caught the warm coconut smell of his skin. "That must have been hard—leaving friends and school and all...."

"You make new friends. I learned to pack light in life."

She thought about how much junk he'd filled the cottage with and wondered what he meant.

"I think it was harder on my sister than me."

"Is this her?" Ariel tapped the girl in the photo.

"Yep. That's Penny."

"She's pretty. Your mother, too."

"Penny's a great kid. If I can keep my parents from squashing her spirit."

"Really?"

"I think they're afraid she'll turn out like me."

"And that's bad?"

"To my folks, yeah. My dad lives to lay down the law. I did okay in school, but not up to muster in his mind. And not only was I not interested in a Navy career, I made it a point to debate military spending at the dinner table."

"Ouch," she said.

"I figured I must have been adopted." He grinned at her, but she saw regret in his eyes. And sadness.

"She looks happy here," Ariel said, picking up another photo of Penny—this one a prom shot with a date.

"Yeah. But she works hard to keep the peace with the folks—and keep me from worrying about her." He studied the photo.

It was sweet that Jake was so concerned about his sister. She noticed a more recent shot of Penny with Jake. His blue eyes gleamed with pleasure and his smile was so wide he had a dimple—as if his face couldn't hold his happiness without crinkling.

"So now you know about my family," Jake said,

drawing her gaze away from the picture. He folded his arms and tilted his head in her direction. "Tell me about yours."

"Not much to tell. My mother lives in Pasadena."

"Brothers and sisters?"

"Nope. It's always been just me and my mom. My dad died when I was three."

"I'm sorry." Jake stood uncomfortably close and studied her face.

She took a step back and bumped into the bureau. "It's all right. I don't remember him. Mom and I were a good team. Us against the world, you know?" She smiled.

"You two still close?"

"Not as much as I'd like. We're both busy. We talk on the phone." She felt a little guilty about that, but with the new business, she'd been obsessed. Troubled by the thought, she focused in on the task at hand. "I'd better let you get back to moving out," she said. "How about if I empty the closet for you?"

"You always in a hurry?" he said.

"That's how I get things done."

"I get the feeling if I don't look out, you'll just mow me down."

"Doesn't seem likely." She knew from crashing into him earlier that she'd just bounce off his powerful frame. The thought gave her a shiver. She tried not to picture herself falling into him anywhere near a bed.

Jake shook his head as though he thought she was crazy, but he did sweep up the shirts from the bed, gather an armful of shoes from the closet and carry the whole mess through the broken wall to the guest room.

Ariel began to hang her dresses, suits and coats in the partially emptied closet, using the metal hangers there. Tomorrow, she'd get her wooden hangers out of storage, along with everything she needed to make the place feel like home. She'd returned to her suitcase and gathered an armload of lingerie when Jake returned.

"What you got there?" he teased.

She clutched her undies to her chest, painfully aware of how many were granny panties.

"I'll show you mine if you show me yours." He opened a bureau drawer and lifted out an armload of socks and underwear—boxers, she noticed—in a riot of colors, many of them silk.

"That's okay," she said, holding her sensible unmentionables more tightly.

"There's nothing wrong with white," he said.

She blushed, then just shoved the clothes into the emptied drawer. She wasn't about to organize them with Jake watching over her shoulder.

"White is a tease," he continued. "Simple and innocent. Take the bra you've got on. It's so thin a guy might think you're not wearing anything at all...just speaking theoretically, of course."

"Of course." She crossed her arms over her chest.

"You have no idea what it does to a man when he thinks a woman has nothing on underneath," he said, watching her face.

She felt an unnerving tickle between her legs, so she turned to grab up more clothes—slips and scarves—from her bag.

She turned back just as he mused, "No snaps, no latches, no hooks.... Just one thin layer of fabric between us and glory." He grabbed some T-shirts from a drawer, emptying it, then grinned at her, "And if there are no panties...well, that's like winning a Powerball."

"What makes you think I want to know this?" she said, shoving her clothes into the emptied space, unhappily close to Jake, who leaned against the bureau.

"Don't women wonder what men think about?"

"We already know—sex...every fifteen seconds, right?" She closed the drawer with an authoritative hip check.

"Well, I don't wear underwear." He winked. "In case you're curious."

She couldn't help glancing at the crotch of his swim trunks. When she dragged her gaze back up, he was waiting for her with a smirk. *Gotcha*.

"Women buy me these," he said, lifting the load in his arms. "God knows why."

Especially because he probably wasted no time getting out of them. He wandered away, Lucky lumbering after him. Ariel watched him go, unable to believe she was joking about underwear with a man she'd only known for four hours.

Her energy seemed to give Jake momentum, at least, and he picked up the pace. While she emptied her second suitcase, Jake dragged the weight bench out, along with some things piled in the corner—a basket with Frisbees and balls and a brightly colored fabric kite—whistling cheerfully the entire time.

Ariel was putting the photo of her and her mother on her nightstand when Jake stopped to look. "Your mom?" he said, picking up the pewter frame and examining its contents. Light flashed from the glass onto his face.

"Yeah. Christmas three years ago." She and her mother stood with their arms around each other's waist in front of the fake Christmas tree in her mother's manufactured home. Myra, one of the diner waitresses, had taken the shot.

"You look like her," Jake said, studying the picture. "Same jaw and mouth. Your eyes are the same green. Nice."

"Thank you." She looked down at the photo again, concentrating on her mother. "She looks tired, don't you think? She worked double shifts to afford this Christmas." That had to stop. Ariel couldn't wait to make enough money to supplement what her mother made at the diner, so she could work part-time, maybe go to school, have some vacation, do something she really wanted besides work, work, work. The thought of that put the fire in Ariel's belly again. She would make this business fly, or die trying.

"So, invite her out here for a weekend," Jake said. "She can hit the beach and relax."

Ariel laughed. "My mother at the beach? I can't imagine." It would be good for her to take a breather, though, and the two of them could do some real talking for a change. Maybe after she'd made some headway with her business and the cottage was finished, she'd invite her mother out to see the place.

Jake put the photo on the bureau, then surveyed the room. "Looks like you're set."

"For now. Tomorrow I'll get my office equipment and personal stuff out of storage. Rent a truck, I guess."

"You need a truck? I can borrow one easy, if you'd like."

She looked at him. Borrowing a truck would be quicker and cheaper. Otherwise, she'd have to take buses to where her car was waiting in a friend's garage, drive to the truck rental place, backtrack to return the truck. "I hate to put you out. You have all the work on the cottage to do."

"I've got plenty of time for that."

"Just a month."

He just grinned, acknowledging her jab, but brushing it off. "Let me give you a hand."

"Okay. I'd appreciate that. I'll pay for gas, of course."

"Come on. We're roommates."

For some reason, they both looked straight at the unmade bed, still dented from her nap. Ariel suddenly needed him out of the gold-lit room that was entirely too intimate for strangers—even strangers who'd examined each other's underwear.

She looked toward what would be Jake's room—for tonight at least—and saw the gaping hole. "Maybe we should put that sheet up now? Between the rooms? Maybe one of those canvas drop cloths would work." *Nice and thick and opaque.*

"You sure? You won't bother me. Unless you walk in your sleep? And that wouldn't necessarily be a problem...." He was teasing her, but she felt that funny quiver all up and down her spine.

"I'm a very quiet sleeper," she said primly. "But I'd like the canvas, please."

"You're the boss," he said and headed away, grinning, Lucky at his heels.

Jake brought back the canvas and Ariel held it up while he nailed it in place. It was thick, but no sound barrier. She thought about telling Jake not to bring Heather home, but decided she'd probably ordered him around enough for the night, and vowed to be asleep before any hanky-panky got started.

A snuffling sound made her turn. There stood Lucky with his head squished into an odd shape, a silky trunk of panty hose hanging from his muzzle. Her last pair of fancy stockings!

"How did you get those?" she asked him, tugging the panty hose off his face and holding them up. "Ruined."

Jake laughed. "That's no way to get into a lady's underwear, Lucky."

"I spent a fortune on these."

"You've got great legs, why cover them up?"

"It's just the principle of the thing," she said, though the compliment was not lost on her. Her fancy nylons were ruined, kind of like her life plan right now. The beach was out to get her one way or another. She balled up the shredded delicate and shot Lucky a fierce look.

Who, me? Lucky's expression seemed to say. Just like Jake.

"Come on, Lucky," Jake said. "I think we just wore out our welcome." He held open the drop-cloth curtain between the bedrooms until Lucky passed over. He hesitated before following. "Holler if you need any more help," he said.

Help? God save her from any more of his help tonight. "I'll be fine, thanks," she said, relieved when he let the cloth barrier fall between them.

4

WHILE ARIEL CAREFULLY FOLDED and organized the unmentionables Jake had repeatedly mentioned, she could hear him clunking around in his room. *White is a tease*, he'd said. *Simple and innocent*. Her cheeks heated. Please. He was just one line after the next.

When she'd finished putting all her things away, she surveyed the room. It needed her pictures on the wall and her rocking chair and her linens, all of which were in storage. But with Jake's truck, she'd be able to pick up everything. That was one thing off her to-do list.

Now to call her mother. She'd alerted her from London that she'd be returning. She tapped in the number, determined to put things in the best possible light so her mother wouldn't worry.

"I'm baaack," she said when her mom picked up.

"I'm so sorry, sweetie. You had your heart set on London."

"But this is a challenge, too," she said. "Building my own business will be fun." Her stomach twisted with tension.

"How's the beach house?"

"Very...beachy. Trudy was having it fixed up. So I'm, um, dealing with that."

"When you set your mind to something, you make it happen. You're like me that way."

"I hope I'm like you."

"Of course you are. Your father was so distractible. Always ready to change directions. You have a good head on your shoulders."

With Jake in the equation, though, Ariel wasn't so sure she could plow through with her usual efficiency.

"What's the matter?" her mother asked.

"Nothing really. The handyman who's doing the work is, uh, living here, too."

"Oh. Well. Is that wise?"

"I don't think so. I've asked him to make other arrangements."

"That's smart. Is he skilled?"

"He seems a tad too easygoing to me, but Trudy says he's good."

"Does she have a contract with him?"

"I don't know. At least I haven't seen one." Jake had probably made a paper boat of it and floated it out on the tide.

"Big mistake with easygoing workmen. I've heard it all at the diner. Pin him down, dear. Get it in writing."

"I'll take care of it, make sure he does what needs doing."

"I have no doubt you will. You're a wonder." Ariel wished she were as confident as her mother about that.

Her mother gave a tired sigh.

"Are you all right, Mom? You sound worn out."

"Long day. I'll just put my feet up," she said. Ariel heard her rustle around. "There, that's better."

Her mother's condition worried her and she remembered what Jake had said. "Why don't you come out to the beach with me?"

"That would be nice, dear," her mother said politely.

"No, I mean let's plan it. Take a Saturday off and spend the day with me. The whole weekend, if you'd like." Jake would be long gone by then.

"We're pretty busy at the diner."

"No one would mind if you took a weekend off."

"Maybe not…" she said. "But what about your business?"

"Everyone needs a break, don't they?" She held her breath.

"I'd like to spend some time with you, but I'm not much of a beach person."

"Neither am I," Ariel said.

"Your father always wanted the beach, but I was not interested. Too much sand and smell."

"I know exactly what you mean." Ariel chuckled at the pair of them. "If we don't want to swim, we can stay on the porch and look out at the water. How about that?"

"Sounds lovely."

Ariel felt the pain of separation like a stab. "So, let's pick a date and you can clear it with everyone." She named the Saturday three weeks away and her mother agreed.

"Now tell me all about your business," her mother said. So Ariel laid out her plan. She'd start with Trudy's list of contacts, touch base with the former Business Advantage clients, especially the ones she'd handled. She'd join a networking group, contact the Small Business Administration about advertising in a newsletter, and more.

As she talked, her confidence rose, and her mother's

support helped, too. As soon as she hung up, she took a moment for a positive visualization, picturing herself making confident phone calls, then meeting with new clients. She imagined the details—the notes she'd refer to, shaking hands when the client agreed to hire her, setting to work on the project.

She could do this. Except not this minute, she realized as exhaustion washed over her. This minute, she should sleep. Tomorrow she'd dig in, bright and fresh.

She gathered her toiletries and her nightgown, a high-necked pink thing that Jake would laugh at since he undoubtedly slept nude, and headed into the bathroom.

The bathroom was a masculine mess—towels mildewing in the corner, a sprinkling of beard shavings in the sink, a sagging shower curtain, Jake's shaving cream, razor, toothpaste and toothbrush scattered everywhere except the dusty toiletry organizer meant to hold them. Only a gooey soap bar rested in its place.

The medicine cabinet held a few items—disposable razors, bandages, antiseptic, liniment, a comb and deodorant. Plenty of room for her cosmetics and creams.

She put her things away, then paused at the sight of Jake's razor on the ledge above the sink. She picked it up and sniffed. Densely sweet coconut. So this was the source of that great smell. She sniffed deeply, guiltily, then rinsed the razor.

Might as well help him a little. She washed the toiletry rack, then put the rinsed-off soap and Jake's razor in place. She neatened the toothpaste tube, locating its cap under the sink, then put it, along with Jake's toothbrush and shaving cream, in the correct spot.

She took Jake's cologne out of the medicine chest and

started to put it in its designated indentation, but that might be too much. She sniffed at the cologne, though. Light, with a bit of musk. Nice.

She picked up the towels Jake had hurled in the corner and hung them over the shower rod so they could dry. Hmm. She'd have to buy a new shower curtain. This one was cloudy with lime, torn from three of its hooks and trimmed in mildew. Beach living. She sighed.

In the next room, she could hear Jake lifting weights, the clank as regular as a clock's tick. The man didn't know how to do anything quietly, did he?

She should have been more firm about him moving out. She'd bet her sensible panties that he'd stretch out those *couple of days* if she allowed it.

The underwear banter had been kind of fun, she had to admit. A sense of humor was important in life. That made her remember her Husband-To-Be Checklist, which she'd put together a couple of years ago with her future in mind. Maybe making a list of criteria for a husband was odd, but goal-setting was the secret to success in life as well as business.

She ran down her list in her mind. *He would be responsible and ambitious and emotionally dependable. He would be thoughtful and a good listener. He would feel her pain as deeply as his own. He would know her, sometimes better than she knew herself.*

Oh, and he'd bring her roses. Romance had a place in love, but not the prime one. You couldn't let romance bewitch you into falling for someone who didn't meet more important criteria.

And he'd have a sense of humor, she added now. How could she have left that off? Of course Jake was the opposite of her dream man in every way—even his blond hair—except for the sense of humor. A sense of humor was important.

The banging and clanking stopped and Jake began to whistle—perfectly tuneful. She hoped her man would have a good voice, though that would be icing on the cake. The main thing was to be compatible, to be partners, looking ahead to the same things, enjoying the same pleasures and plans.

"Come on, pal," she heard Jake call. Lucky barked. Then she heard the door open and close. Jake was off to the volleyball game and Heather. She felt strangely alone. Jake Renner did fill up a space.

On the other hand, with him out of the house, she felt more comfortable wearing her nightgown around. She was so tired, she was tempted to skip her nightly routine, but if you dropped good habits over a little jet lag, who knew where that could lead?

So she washed and moisturized her face, using a circular massage to enhance circulation, gave her hair the required hundred strokes and brushed and flossed her teeth.

Finished, she made her way to the bed, cuddling into the pillow, intent on falling so deeply asleep she'd miss any post-volleyball action beyond the canvas screen.

ARIEL WOKE WITH A START and shot to a sit. Her clock said midnight. She'd only slept three hours. Of course, it was 8:00 in the morning in London, which probably explained why she'd awakened. She decided to make herself some tea. That was one memory of England she'd carried home—several tins of fabulous tea, which she'd stored above the stove in the kitchen.

She tiptoed down the hall, trying to minimize the wooden floor's creak. Jake's door was closed, but she held her breath. She'd show by example how to be courteous to someone sleeping.

In the kitchen, she turned on the stove light and located the tea. Without so much as a clunk, she put a saucepan of water on to boil. She yawned. It would take a few days to get back on track sleep-wise from the time change, though sleep was often elusive when she was worried, and she was very worried.

She leaned over the hissing pot, letting the steam warm her face. Soothing. She'd get through this one task at a time. She poured the bubbling water into a mug where she'd placed a bag of chamomile and mint, and breathed in the rich aroma...and thought of London.

How she missed it. Even the relentless dreariness of the weather had not put a dent in her pleasure. All gone now—fizzled like the last bit of an Alka-Seltzer tablet. She'd go back one day, once her business took off, maybe with her husband...yes, before they had the first of their two children.

She clutched the mug between her palms, close to her face and carried it to the kitchen table. Out the window, she saw that the full moon glimmered on the ocean. The waves shushed in the distance.

For the first time, it struck her how lovely this was. A person could stare at the ocean for hours. The sound of the waves was soothing, almost hypnotic. Then she caught movement in the water. A huge fish...? No. A person. Swimming in the moonlight along the shore with long, strong strokes. A man, judging by the length of the arms and what seemed to be a bare upper body. After a bit, he flipped over and floated on his back, staring up at the sky. It must be cold, she thought, and swimming in the dark would be scary. On the other hand, people paid big bucks to have a house at the beach so they could do things like swim at night.

Not her, though.

Under the moon's glow, the swimmer looked mysterious, ephemeral—like some creature in a sea myth—a sea god or ghost. Strange.

Her gaze caught on a smear of mildew in the caulking on the window ledge. Following it upward, she spotted wood rot at the top of the window frame. That would need to be fixed. She took a deep breath and blew it out, then took another warm swallow of tea. *Relax, go easy.* Now, when she couldn't shut down for sleep, she saw the appeal of taking life as easy as Jake did.

Since she was awake, she might as well get started on her task lists. She tiptoed back to her room for the notepad from her purse, returned to the table and started. First, *pick up things from storage.* Here, she was dependent on Jake and his friend's truck. She'd try to get that going as early as possible. Hard to be pushy when someone was doing you a favor.

Next, *purchase office supplies, order new business cards and stationery.* Minimal amounts, to keep costs down. *Get a second phone line for business?* No, not yet. Too expensive. She couldn't even afford her cell phone after tomorrow. *Work Trudy's contact list.* She'd do that before or after getting things out of storage. Maybe both.

She had to make things work right away. Anxiety

tightened her chest. *Keep on keeping on.* She had enough savings for a couple of months. If clients didn't come right away, she'd get a job at a temp agency. Except how could she build a business when she was only available in the evenings? Part-time consultants did not inspire confidence....

Blood pounded in her head. Her stomach knotted. The business items were not helping her relax, so she started on her personal to-dos, turning to a fresh page. *Change the utilities and trash pick-up accounts to her name, file ownership papers on the house, devise a budget. Pin Jake down about moving out.*

Thinking of Jake made her jumpier than ever. She flipped her notepad shut and looked out the window for the swimmer. Gone. Probably off to sleep like a normal person. Ariel should try sleeping again. First, she'd clear the painting junk away from one side of the living room, where she'd set up her office in the morning.

She rose from the kitchen table to head to the living room, and stopped in shock. A man stood outside the kitchen door on the sun porch. Her heart flew into her throat and she froze, unable to make a sound.

The door opened.... She tried to move, to shout, to do something. Then she saw it was Jake—soaking wet, dripping on the floor, a towel around his neck. He was her mysterious moonlight swimmer.

"You scared me to death!" she said, pressing her hand to her thudding heart.

"What are you doing up?" He scrubbed his hair with the towel, the moonlight playing on the planes of his face and the shifting muscles of his arms.

"The time lag from London, I guess. That was you out there swimming?"

"Yeah. I had energy and it's a great moon." He came closer. In the dim light, he seemed like someone who'd stepped out of a dream, not quite real. "It's more than the time lag," he said, taking in her face. "You're doing that thing with your lip."

"What thing?"

"Chewing on it. Like for dinner. What's going on?"

"Nothing. I just have a lot on my mind." She didn't realize she'd made biting her lip a habit. For all his laid-back attitude, Jake didn't seem to miss much.

"I know exactly what you need. Go get your suit."

"My suit?"

"Yeah, we'll go for a swim."

"But you just swam. And it's dark and cold and—"

"Perfect. Night swimming is the best. It's just what you need to put you to sleep. Trust me."

"I'm not that strong a swimmer." In the ocean anyway. The thought of what might be cruising around in the dark out there, what currents and undertows and creatures might be lying in wait...

"I'll keep an eye on you." He winked. "Go get your suit. Or, come to think of it, who needs suits?" He made as if to remove his trunks.

"No, no. I'll get my suit," she said. While she scrambled into her modest one-piece, hopping on first one foot, then the other, she argued with herself. *This is insane. It's the middle of the night. There could be sharks.* Followed by *Oh, lighten up. Be spontaneous for once. Maybe Jake's right and this will make you sleepy.*

Dressed, she glanced at her face in the mirror—pale, excited and scared. Was she losing her mind?

Jake met her at the kitchen door, and they headed across the porch and down the stairs. The May night was pleasant—warm with a light breeze. The sand tickled her insteps, shifted under her in that irritating way sand had, but she stayed on the balls of her feet and scampered to keep up with Jake's long strides. Soon they reached wet sand, which was easier to cross—flat and elastic, almost alive. And not too cold.

But the water, when they reached it, was icy. Ariel shrieked, then covered her mouth.

"Scream freely," Jake said. "You won't bother anybody."

She saw he was right. The beach was empty for as far as she could see in either direction, glowing a ghostly white in the moonlight. The houses and condos were dark except for a few windows shining yellow from lamplight or blue from a TV.

The water lapped at her ankles. She hugged herself and backed away. "Too cold."

"Come on," Jake said, starting forward, reaching a hand back for her.

She shook her head and backed up.

"Jump in, get it over with," Jake said, standing in water up to his waist. He turned, dove in, swam a few feet away, then returned.

Goaded by his grin, Ariel moved gingerly forward, gasping as the water slid like bands of ice up her calves, then her thighs. "I don't know about this," she said, wondering what that bumpy thing she was stepping on was, praying it wouldn't bite or slice her foot.

"Sure you do," Jake said. He marched through the water to her, then swung her into his arms. She gasped. His wet chest was cold against her skin. "What are you doing?"

He carried her deeper into the water.

"Put me down."

"You sure?" he said and dropped her with a splash.

She came up shrieking, gasped for air and slugged his arm. "That was mean."

"But you got it over with. See how nice it is now?" He bobbed near where she stood with the water up to her neck.

"I prefer to ease into things," she said, surprised to find the water wasn't so cold after all. He was right, damn him.

"I bet you take a bandage off hair by hair, too."

"As a matter of fact, I do," she said.

"Too much agony that way." He rolled onto his back. "Ain't this the life?"

She looked across the sea. The dark expanse of water seemed threatening and overwhelming. But right here close to Jake, the sea was silky and the waves produced a gentle, comforting sway, rocking her closer to, then away from Jake. She rolled onto her back the way Jake was doing and stared up at the sky, a black blanket, the stars dimmed by the thick ocean air.

"It is kind of nice," she admitted, her words sounding muffled in her water-filled ears. She turned to the side and caught Jake watching her. Their gazes locked and energy rolled between them like the waves they were swaying in. Startled, she went under.

Jake pulled her up quickly. "You okay?" he said, gripping her by both upper arms.

"Fine," she said, still caught by the energy between them.

"You look like you belong in the water," he said softly.

"I doubt that." Jake did, though. He seemed like a sea being, putting her under a spell, luring her near, pulling her in. The shifting water rocked her closer and closer. *Go there, it's magic, it's right*...the wave seemed to say. Hazily, she realized she was moving closer, hypnotized by the moment, the look on Jake's face, the suspended dream of it all.

"Quit it," he murmured.

"Quit what?" she murmured back.

"You're chewing your lip again," he said, moving closer.

"I am?" she said, swaying nearer.

"Yeah. And I have a much better idea for your mouth."

"Like what?" she breathed.

"Like this..." he said and when he moved in to touch his salt-flavored lips to hers, she wasn't the least surprised.

Heat shot through her and she made a sound. Jake pulled her gently against him, his tongue just there, soft and waiting. Waiting for her to open up to him...to this experience...to...

Pure insanity.

Ariel broke off the kiss and sloshed away from Jake. "You said you never sleep with roommates," she managed to say, forcing indignation into her tone.

Jake shrugged. "I'm moving out, remember?"

"This is a bad idea. My life is upside down right now. I need all my concentration..."

"*All* your concentration?"

She gulped. "I'm very busy." Too busy for Jake's mouth, Jake's arms and a few incredible hours in Jake's bed? Her wild side was hopping around like a child fighting to escape from the time-out corner.

"You're sooo strict," he said, shaking his head, his eyes laughing, but she could see he accepted her decision.

"Somebody has to be," she said, backing away from him to keep herself from just surging into his arms.

"You're leaving? But we're not done swimming."

"I'm done," she said. Done swimming in lust-infested waters anyway. "And I need some sleep."

"We could do that, too."

"No thanks," she said, continuing her backward walk. "The point was to get me relaxed. And I am. Very relaxed." Before he could contradict her, she turned to plow to the shore.

Relaxed? Ariel asked herself lying miserably in her bed a few minutes later. She'd barely rinsed off the sand in the shower and hurried to her room to avoid another encounter with Jake. The last thing she felt was *relaxed*. She could still feel Jake's lips on hers—warm and strong and ready for whatever she wanted. Her whole body seemed alive with what she wanted. She touched her fingers to her still-tingling lips. She thought of Jake's eyes on her, watching her with that curious combination of concern and appreciation, as the waves swelled and dipped around them, feeling that magical sense that they belonged together there. Hell. She was going as wonky as poor Trudy.

But that was just the Jake routine, she told herself. Just standard practice with women. *How about a night swim, baby?* He probably always tried that one.

She heard him come into the house, then silence. She turned on her side, fighting for sleep. Finally, finally, she felt herself drift off…

Bang…clunk…crash…bang. Jake was hammering something to a wall or a door. Then there was a ripping sound. What? He was working on the house now? In the middle of the night?

She could go out there and yell at him, but who knew where that might lead? Instead, she groaned and folded the pillow over her ears. At least he was working. The sooner he finished the cottage, the sooner he'd be completely out of her hair.

THERE WAS SOMETHING about that woman, Jake thought, trying to understand why he'd kissed her when everything in him said it was a bad idea. She'd looked so good in the water—softer, more womanly, less bristly. Limber as a seal, too, with an easy grace she didn't know she had. The feeling had caught him off guard, like an unexpected wave, and he'd wanted to hold her just to feel all that electric energy against his skin, taste it with his tongue.

What a pistol. Jake's mother's expression for someone full of sparks and fire fit Ariel Adams to a T. Even exhausted from lack of sleep, she fairly glowed with energy. She made him want to blink and step back.

And she practically screamed *help me relax*—from her

tight little 'do, to her buttoned-up suit, forward-leaning walk and no-nonsense mouth. She reminded him of the businesswomen who sometimes landed on one of his sailboat charters—wound too tight, clutching their cell phones like security blankets, wanting to stay on top and in control.

He liked how the slow, easy energy of a sail gradually took over and relaxed them, until they let go like a twisted rope flung free. Loosening up Ariel Adams, however, would take more than a day on the ocean, he suspected.

But he couldn't sleep with her. She was right about that. If ever there was any woman who would make sex complicated, it would be Ariel. Staying at the beach house was about keeping his living costs down...and maybe having a little fun—like taking Ariel swimming tonight. Maybe he'd teach her to sail or dive. He'd be helping her. It was practically a public service. He rolled his eyes at himself.

He already knew one way to her heart was cooking, so he intended to make her mouthwatering meal after mouthwatering meal until she wanted him around for that alone.

For now, he'd see about turning the sunporch into an office. That would satisfy her workaholism and take the pressure off him to move out of the room she wanted.

The tattered screens came off easily. By the time he'd taken measurements for Plexiglas replacements, it was 3:00 a.m. so he went to bed. He had to get up at a decent time to make her a nice breakfast and convince her he was the best roommate she could ever want.

5

ARIEL WOKE the next morning to her alarm and the mouthwatering smell of something baking. She'd slept through Jake's banging, thanks to her pillow, but she was still groggy after so little sleep. She forced herself to sit up.

She'd make calls before they went to pick up her things at the storage place. And she *had* to make sure Jake knew that the kiss had been a late-night mistake. She threw on her robe and headed for the bathroom, only to run headlong into Jake, who held out a plate brimming with fresh fruit and a steaming muffin. "Breakfast is served," he said with a slight bow.

"You shouldn't have. Really."

"You need your strength." He stood there holding the plate looking fresh and healthy and bare-chested—were those Hawaiian shirts for show like his boxers?—on less sleep than she'd had.

The muffin smelled so good. Was he going to bring the plate for her to eat in bed? "I'll come into the kitchen," she said, clutching her robe closed. She backed into the bathroom.

"Nice nightgown," he said, his eyes twinkling.

She looked down at the polyester ruffles. "Simple and innocent?" she joked back.

"For a grandma, maybe." He fingered the ruffle high on her neck. "I see you in sheer white silk."

Her cheeks heated and she made to close the door.

"Okay, but don't dawdle. These are best when they're still warm." He wiggled the muffin under her nose, then backed down the hall, as if luring her with the food.

Of course, it worked. She did the essentials, threw on some jeans shorts and a tank top, then headed into the kitchen like Lucky on the trail of fresh bacon. She was a sucker for fresh-baked goods. She hoped her metabolism could handle a day or two of Jake's cooking.

She found Jake waiting for her at the kitchen table. He motioned for her to sit where he'd placed the plate of muffin and fruit—a small heap of raspberries, triangles of fresh pineapple and slices of mango and papaya.

She plunked into the chair and Jake tore open the muffin, cupped half in his palm and lovingly covered it with butter, which melted into its fluffy center.

Ariel had to suck up saliva to keep from drooling. "Jake, this really isn't necessary. I—"

"Eat," he said and lifted the muffin to her mouth. Of course she took a bite. The muffin dissolved on her tongue, each blueberry a tangy surprise. "Mmm," she couldn't help moaning, embarrassed at how sexual that sounded. "So good."

"The secret's sour cream," he said.

She took the buttered muffin from his hand and consumed another bite.

He watched her fondly, his chin resting on his palm.

"Really, you can't fuss like this," she said. As long as she was hungry, he could have his way with her with cooking.

"It's no more than I'd do for Lucky."

"Right." When was the last time he'd kissed a dog? Fighting the urge to gulp more muffin, she decided to clear the air. "Jake, about last night, I just want you to know…"

"It's fine. I understand. Look what I did." He stood and went to fling open the kitchen door. "Voila! Your new office."

She saw that the screens on the sunporch had been torn from the windows and lay in a tangled pile on the sandy porch floor. "My office?"

"Yeah. I got started on it last night."

"But now there's nothing to keep out the sand."

"I'll get the Plexiglas up, no sweat, and you'll have an office with a million-dollar view."

"I told you I can't afford anything extra." Her annoyance didn't keep her from wolfing down the other half of the muffin.

"My friends will do me a deal on the glass. And my labor—" he waggled his brow "—you and I can work out some kind of trade." He returned to sit across from her.

"What does that mean?" she said, the muffin turning to sawdust on her tongue. "What kind of trade?"

"Hard to say. Try the raspberries." He forked a few and aimed them at her mouth. "Maybe I need some business advice." If only his eyes didn't seem so honest, so open, so full of fun.

"You're not even in a business."

"Good point. But maybe someday I'll get the urge to get a j-o-b." He pretended to shudder.

"What's wrong with a job?"

"Takes too big a bite out of my day."

"Brother. Aren't you going to eat?"

"I already have. Finish up so we can go for a quick swim."

"No thanks." She wasn't climbing into the ocean with him again. Swimming and kissing were getting all mixed up in her mind. "Besides, you're not supposed to swim for forty-five minutes after eating."

"An exaggeration. Check the research. You're eating light."

"I need to get busy. And, on that subject, will your friend loan us that truck this morning? Soon?"

"I'll give him a call. Come swimming. This is your first day. The work will still be there when you're done swimming."

"And the swimming will still be there when I'm done working." The raspberries were so sweet. Then she moved on to the papaya and decided it was the best yet. Except for that muffin. She took another bite of that.

"Come on, Ariel. You're living on the beach. It's no accident that philosophers use the sea to put life's little problems in perspective. Water wearing away sharp edges, waves ebbing and flowing, the daily rhythm of the tide."

"The best way to put life's little problems in perspective is to tackle them head-on, not wait for waves to wash them out to sea."

He laughed and shook his head as if she was crazy.

"I didn't choose to live on the beach, you know. I was forced here."

"Maybe the beach chose you. Maybe that's why you're here."

Brother. Zen Master Beach Bum. Though something

told her this laid-back, no-sweat attitude wasn't as natural to Jake as he made it seem. There was sharp intellect behind those smoky blue eyes. He was deliberately underachieving for some reason. She felt a stab of curiosity about the Jake who lived behind the Mr. Affable facade, but the less she thought about the man, the better.

"Trudy chose the beach, not me," she said. "And I'm here because she felt guilty."

"Guilty?" Jake asked.

She finished chewing, nodding her head all the while. "Yeah. We had the perfect plan to work together for two years until I was ready to go off on my own."

"What happened?"

"Trudy fell in love." She shook her head.

"And that's a bad thing?"

"In this case, the worst. Trudy stayed in London with the man she fell for and turned the remains of her business and this house over to me. It means starting up on my own, which I'm not ready for. As for love, I think it's always bad when the timing's wrong."

"You can't time love, Ariel."

Oh, yes I can. She looked up at him. "You're quite the philosopher. Have you ever been in love?"

"A few times."

"But you never got serious?"

"No."

"You will eventually, right?"

He shrugged.

"You're waiting for the timing to be right—my point exactly."

"I'm not putting it on my calendar," he said. "If it doesn't happen, so be it."

"Refusing to plan is planning."

"Now who's the philosopher? And what about you? You been in love?"

"Once," she said, though it was probably a mistake to confess this to Jake. "In college. But we were too young...." She'd completely lost her head, fallen head over heels for Grayson, a photojournalist ambitious for adventure. She'd become obsessed with him, made wild plans to put her degree on hold to travel the world with him on assignment. Then Grayson had come to his senses, realized they were rushing things, tying each other down, blah, blah, blah. It had hurt like hell, but it was like ice water splashed in the face of a hysterical person—the sharp shock of reality.

"And you don't want to get hurt like that again?" Jake said, breaking into her memory.

"Who says I got hurt?"

"Your eyes, I guess. Something sad in there."

The man was way too perceptive. Or she was too transparent. "I just came to my senses. It was an anomaly."

"An anomaly? So love's a statistical error? You fell for a guy. What's wrong with that?"

"Everything. For me, at that time." It had been a lesson in watching over her heart, guarding against the part of her that wanted to run and play, go with the moment, be impulsive. The part of her that came from her spontaneous father, not her sensible, practical mother.

"How about you?" she asked, moving on to the slices of mango—even better than the papaya. "Ever have your heart broken?" The pineapple wasn't bad either.

"Feelings change. Things run their course." But he looked guilty as hell.

"In other words, you've never been dumped." No surprise. She'd seen that barrier between him and poor Heather.

"I guess not."

"So you keep things light, right? Nothing exclusive and no long affairs? So the women never get the wrong idea?"

"You got me," he said, looking sheepish.

For some reason, she couldn't resist a jab. Maybe she'd been a little more hurt by Grayson than she wanted to admit. "Great sex, enjoy the moment, we only have today?"

"You're good," he said, but his loose smile had tightened.

"No, you're just obvious."

Hurt flickered across his face. She'd gone too far. "That was rude. I'm just upset over Trudy and her nutty love affair."

"No prob," he said, shrugging off the hurt the way Lucky shed sand. For a moment, she envied him that easy release of feelings. "And I'm sorry you lost your partner. That could throw anyone."

"Yeah. Thanks."

"You're doing it again."

"What?"

"Slicing and dicing your bottom lip," he said, watching her closely. That reminded her of the alternate lip activity he'd suggested last night in the ocean. Her face heated.

"You'll do fine without a partner," he said. "You have a determined glint in your eye."

She arched a brow at him. "I have a glint? Would you trust a consultant with a glint?" She was trying to joke, but it didn't come out sounding funny.

"I'd trust you," he said simply.

She smiled at him, grateful, even though he was completely full of it. An unusual intimacy had sprung up between them. They'd had a personal conversation about love and hurt and she was mystified about how it had happened, except it had something to do with a fresh-baked, hand-fed muffin. And Jake.

"Don't let me keep you from your swim," she said. "I need to get busy."

He zeroed in on her face. "Things will work out, Ariel."

"You make it sound easy."

"I didn't say it will be easy. I just said it will work out. Sure you won't swim with me?"

"Not this morning." Or ever.

"Then I'll take a run, I guess," he said. He was up from the table and out the kitchen door before she knew it. She found herself standing and trailing him until she stood on the messy sunporch and watched him through the empty window frames. "What about the truck?" she shouted to him.

He turned, jogging in place. "When I get back. No sweat!" he called, then ran off.

He looked so good running. He held himself high and tight, yet his joints stayed loose, and his hair bounced on his shoulders, glinting silver in the sun. Ariel's heart leaped, watching him, and she wanted to just run after him, her legs stretching, muscles pumping, too, the breeze in her face. But that was escapism. You didn't get anywhere running off to play any time you felt like it. There would be plenty of time for aerobic exercise once she got things under control.

Right now, she'd fire up the laptop and start making calls until Jake returned. Though she didn't have a minute to waste, she stood watching Jake get smaller in the distance. She made out a dog—Lucky—galloping up to him. Even from this distance she could hear the joy in his bark. Two women in bikinis approached. Jake ran in place while they talked, one of them touching his arm, standing very close.

They all knew Jake, she'd bet, the free-and-easy women on the beach. Didn't they have jobs? This was a weekday, for heaven's sake, and here they were, strolling in the sand.

Get busy, Ariel told herself sternly, taking a deep breath, bracing herself to dig in. She reentered the kitchen. What a mess. Did Jake have to splatter batter everywhere? She gritted her teeth and headed for her computer. She'd clean up when it was time for a break.

Listening to her laptop hum to life, she felt her heart kick up. So much depended on how this went. Soliciting clients was Trudy's area of expertise. Once Ariel started working with a client, she was gold. But this part—convincing them they needed her—this was intimidating. *Push through*, she told herself. *Feel the fear and do it anyway.* Cheap advice from a self-help book, but any port in a storm.

She opened Trudy's business-leads software and read over the list, studying the notes Trudy had included with each entry. *Armbruster Restaurant Management. Neil Armbruster, owner. Entrepreneur's Conference, 3/02. Wants more unity among staff. Consider offering training, working up a mission statement.*

Ariel could do that. Easy. She thought about Wendy's Cookies, the mail-order cookie manufacturer she'd helped transform from a small retail shop to a corporate sales concern. She'd helped Wendy create a virtual army of single-minded baker/marketers among her small staff.

She smiled, remembering the reception in the newly opened corporate sales office. *You really understood us,* Wendy had said to Ariel. *You did what we needed, not some cookie cutter model.* They laughed at the pun, but that was Ariel's strength—and why Trudy had wanted her as a partner—her ability to see each client with fresh eyes, to customize her services to suit them.

She'd do that for Neil Armbruster. Armbruster would be first. A for Adams and Armbruster. Ariel picked up the phone and pushed in the numbers, her mind racing. Be confident and enthusiastic, remember what you have to offer. Dizzy, she paused before the last number.

Calm down. You're good. Just get in the door. Maybe a visualization would help.

She hung up and leaned back in her chair to think about her goal—an office in Thousand Oaks, near where she would live eventually. Something with a view, but not too expensive. A reception area, small kitchen. A large window office for her, a smaller one for her associate and access to a conference room for her seminars. She would get there. It was just a matter of time and hard work. And it all started with this first call.

Go time. Ariel clicked the digits and with one efficient receptionist transfer, she had Armbruster on the line.

"Ariel Adams, Business Advantage. Is this a good time?"

"I've got a moment," he said, but someone was talking to him in the background.

"I believe you met my former partner at a conference a while back. Trudy Walters?"

"Walters…? I remember her. Sure. Strategic planning, something like that."

"Exactly. We—I mean, I—specialize in customized planning. I believe Trudy was talking to you about your staff…some issues about training and unity? I know she didn't have a chance to get back to you, so I'm doing that now. I'm hoping we can get together to talk about how I might assist you as you address these issues."

"I don't know, Amy. This is a busy time for us." He muttered something to the person with him.

"Which makes it even more important to have you and your staff on the same page, working together. It's Ariel, by the way. My name. Anyway, our philosophy at Business Advantage is 'go slow to go fast,' meaning that time invested in planning up front makes the decision-making and action stages go more smoothly. Rush the planning and you lose money, good employees and customer loyalty. I—"

"I'm sure you're right, Adrienne."

"Ariel."

"Right. We're managing fine for now. Thanks for calling. Maybe send me a card and I'll keep you in mind."

"If I could just meet you for lunch, take a few notes, maybe I could sketch out a brief proposal at no charge, just so you can see the advantage of my approach. That's why we named our company Business Advantage, actually, because of the advantage we offer our clients."

"Very nice. I think I'll pass right now."

"I understand. I *will* send you a packet, though, so look it over and I'll give you a call in, say, a month? Remember we fit any budget."

"Certainly. Fine." Now his voice held a chill.

She was about to get the telemarketer brush-off. She'd bungled the pitch. "Thank you for your time, Neil. I hope we'll work together one day soon," she said, then finished with their slogan. "And when you think business, think Business Advantage."

"You bet, Erin," Armbruster said on a sigh and hung up before she could correct her name again.

Ariel fought discouragement. Should she have backed down at his first hesitation? No. Persistence was key, Trudy had said in her last you-can-do-it pep talk in London. *Gentle* persistence.

She'd been gentle, right? But the slogan had been overkill. Oh, hell. She typed up the results of the call, then went to the next name on the list—*Kids' World...growing childcare business. Owner...Rachel Hardy. Forty-ish, two kids of her own. Ready for expansion. Wants a family-friendly company. Suggest staff retreat to devise a vision statement and core values.*

Ariel took a deep breath, closed her eyes, visualized the conversation to a successful conclusion, then dialed the number. She'd barely gotten into her pitch when Rachel Hardy interrupted her to say she was about to sell the company. *Okay, no problem.* Ariel made a note to call the new owner in a month.

Next there was a law firm, followed by a chain of martial arts studios, a growing electronics firm, a sign-making company and a wellness center. All dead ends. Then two disconnected phones.

Two more to try and that would be the last of Trudy's leads. Ariel's heart tightened. *Don't panic.* Her next task would be to call their former clients, focusing on the ones she'd worked with, to see if they needed help or could refer her to other companies. After that she'd have to really start cold. A flutter of despair shot through her and she realized she was chewing her lip again.

Forcing a smile on her face—a smile shows in your voice—she made the last two calls. A "maybe" and an "out of town for two weeks." Okay. It was a start. She put down the phone and realized she was dripping with anxious sweat. And she'd only been at this for an hour.

Jake should return any minute and they'd get her things out of storage. In the meantime, she'd clean up the kitchen. Under the sink she found a glorious cache of cleaning products and set to work....

Forty-five minutes later, she was oiling the antique wooden table when Jake returned, his faced flushed, his upper body gleaming with perspiration.

"What the hell happened?" Jake said, surveying the living room and kitchen, hands on his hips, looking baffled.

She followed his gaze. Every surface not covered by drop cloths gleamed. "I cleaned up a bit."

"It smells like a hospital in here."

"That's the chlorine in the mildew remover." She'd had time to rearrange the items in the cupboards so they made more sense, and cleared a space in the living room for her temporary office.

"A bit? I think those white cupboards used to be blue."

"So, can we get the truck now?"

"Absolutely. Let's go before you alphabetize the spices."

She glanced at her watch. "I'd like to be back by two so I can make some more calls."

"Whatever." Jake looked dazed by the improvements.

She grabbed a clipboard, paper and a pen, so she could make notes for the promotional brochure for which she'd want quotes from former clients. When they got back, she'd start on those calls. She was being efficient, at least.

Until she put herself in laid-back Jake's hands. He was helpful, of course. Strong as an ox, he effortlessly loaded the furniture and boxes from the storage spaces into the truck, but he did it in the most leisurely way.

She curbed her natural inclination to issue time-saving orders and tried gentle suggestions. Jake rolled his eyes all the same. Eventually they finished, but her nerves were frazzled and her lip mangled. Then she made the mistake of mentioning she needed office supplies, and Jake insisted on taking her to the store, where he comparison shopped pointlessly with a pretty clerk, while Ariel grabbed computer paper, file folders and other goods.

Then he wanted to stop for lunch—she had to eat sometime, didn't she?—at his favorite falafel stand, where he helped a guy who needed advice on surfing spots. Then he took the long way home in order to show her Playa Linda's best deli, a seafood place with all-you-can-eat shrimp, the best-stocked video place, a bar with great live music and another with unbelievably cheap beer.

He seemed to think he was helping her feel at home, but each moment put her into a tighter knot. The bumpy truck made it difficult to write, but she managed to make a few shaky notes.

When they finally off-loaded the last box at the cottage, it was four-thirty. She should be able to make at least two calls before five. She went straight for the phone.

"Come with me to take the truck back to Ed," Jake said. "He's got a great garden. We can sling back a brew and hang."

"I have calls to make," she said.

"Come on. The work day's over."

"Not yet," she said grimly, looking at her watch. "I have twenty-six minutes." She'd never sleep tonight if she didn't accomplish something. Without even pausing for courage, she dialed Wendy's Cookies...and got voicemail.Wendy had gone for the day. She left a detailed message and hung up to find Jake standing behind her, holding out a beer. "Drink. It'll take the edge off your voice."

"Edge? I have an edge?" she asked, hearing it herself. "An edge and a glint...doesn't sound good." She took the beer and a long swallow.

"I think the idea is to *attract* business, not tackle it to the ground."

She forced herself not to snap at him—he was trying

to be helpful—and said, "How about if you stick with construction, and I'll handle my business?"

"Ouch," he said with a fake wince. Then he grinned and left her standing there holding a beer, watching the muscles of his behind clench and release as he headed away. She took a long, slow swallow of beer. What the heck was wrong with her?

She was still staring after him when he returned with one of his surfboards. "Great waves right now. Care to come with? I could teach you."

"No thanks," she said. "I've got an office to organize."

"Free lessons...roommate special."

"Thanks, but no." The day she took surfing lessons from Jake was the day pigs flew...or she developed a death wish.

"Another time then," he said and trotted down the porch stairs and across the beach, the board under his arm, looking like a poster boy for California sun and fun.

Ariel took another long swig of beer and turned to the phone. Except it was five after five. No more calls today. She wanted to blame Jake, but Jake was just being Jake. She'd voluntarily put herself in his hands and he'd dragged her into his surfer dude time-space continuum. She realized that not only had she accomplished little today, Jake hadn't lifted a trowel on the cottage or made a call about another place to live.

She tried to think calming thoughts of oceans and timelessness and how things just worked out. But she wasn't Jake and for her nothing worked that way.

6

AFTER SOME DAMN FINE SURFING, Jake took the truck back, then caught up with Brice and his buds for some poker and big talk on *Lady's Day*, Brice's boat. He worked for Brice at his shop, Water Gear, teaching scuba and sailboarding, captaining charters and manning the cash register on the rare occasions Brice would leave his pride and joy in someone else's hands.

Around nine, content with a hundred in winnings and the light buzz from the Coronas he'd drunk, Jake headed home. Brice had offered him two new charter gigs. That was good. His income had gotten erratic lately. He'd have to hustle to keep busy through the month. And where *would* he live when he finished the cottage? Now and then the idea of a j-o-b like he'd joked about to Ariel almost sounded like a relief. Those were the moments when he wondered if he was losing his edge.

Then he would think of his dad's harangues about stability and dependability and *locking on your target*, and he'd feel that stubborn need to throw open all the doors, consider a myriad of choices, take nothing for granted—anything to avoid becoming the grim, duty-bound rock his father was. Hell, maybe he'd move to Florida—once he got Penny's trip squared away, that is. Lots of charters in Florida. His friend Dave talked about it all the time.

His life was fine. If he ever doubted it, he could imagine life as his roommate lived it. Anxious and frantic, afraid to rest for one minute. Work was her god. He could never live like that. Even if he did give up and get a job—teaching or something that fit his recreation education degree—he'd make sure to enjoy life. Ariel fought enjoyment like it was dangerous.

He wondered if she was asleep by now. All that nervous energy surely had worn her out. She was so jumpy it put his teeth on edge.

When they'd picked up her junk from storage, she was trying to be polite when she made her "suggestions" and "recommendations" and "it might be more efficient ifs," but the way she chewed her lip, gritted her teeth and the sparks in her eyes told him she was dying to issue a few commands. "Put that here, this there and make it snappy." God, he'd wanted to just kiss her into oblivion...or a different kind of energy anyway.

Instead, he'd deliberately slowed down, teaching her by example how to relax. He'd shown her the high points of town, but her smile looked pasted on the whole time.

She was her own worst enemy. And very different from the women he spent time with. His women traveled light in life. They had jobs, mostly, not careers. A few were models or flight attendants with free time to spend on the beach and superficial interests. They liked company for dinner and clubbing—he was a decent dancer—and easy conversations. The sex was pleasant and varied. And that was fine with him.

Ariel, on the other hand, was a force—always in motion. Headed somewhere. She didn't care if it was the wrong where, she was headed there. He frowned. He wasn't sure he liked coming home to bustle and rush in the beach house.

On the other hand, he kind of liked that she'd spiffed up the place. He didn't mind order—he just didn't see it as worth his time. He realized he was picking up speed, hurrying home in case she was still awake. It bugged him the way his body paid attention to her whenever she was around. The appeal of the forbidden, no doubt.

He found Ariel asleep in her "office" in the front room, her cheek on her desk, lamplight spilling over her dark hair, giving it streaks of golden brown. Her perfume rose to him, a light floral something that hung in his head.

She'd set up her desk and bookcase, filled it with books and binders, had her computer in place, moved the kitchen phone onto the desk. Hell, she even had file folders all labeled. He'd tried to tell her to wait until he got the sunporch done, but she wouldn't hold still. All his construction gear was lined up against the far wall in what looked like height order. Lord.

Maybe he'd be better off moving out, rather than put up with this little control fiend. Except she looked so cute, her hair curving across her pale face, her hands resting on the desk, a pen under one. She'd fallen asleep still working. The lamplight glowed on her unpainted nails and graceful fingers.

He angled his head to read what she'd been writing. Looked like two lists—"business to-do" and "personal to-do." Near the bottom of the personal list, written in all caps, he made out the words, *Pin Jake down about mov-*

ing out. Tighten construction timetable. With several excla-
mation marks.

Lord, he'd made her list of chores. He was a little
wounded. He'd done nothing but cater to the woman
and all she wanted was him done and out.

He caught sight of his name at the bottom of the personal list—*get Jake thank-you gift,* followed by a reggae
band he loved and an album he didn't yet have. She'd
perused his CD collection—probably alphabetized it,
while she was at it. Still, that was thoughtful of her.

Then he saw the last thing on her to-do list—*Don't let
fear rule. Keep on keeping on*—and his heart filled with ten-
derness. The poor thing had fallen asleep making some
frantic list of what she had to do, scared to death the
whole time.

He pulled up a chair to watch her breathe. In sleep,
the tension in her face eased and he saw that her cheeks
were round and smooth as a young girl's. Her lashes
formed dark semi-circles on her cheekbones and her
eyelids quivered—she was dreaming. Probably something terrible about sand blowing into her fax machine.
She had a long, delicate neck and he watched her pulse
beat in the soft hollow at the base of her throat. He had
the sudden urge to press his lips there, feel the beat of
her heart against his mouth.

As if she'd sensed his thoughts, her eyes flew open
and she sat up, the paper sticking to her cheek. "Oh.
Jake," she said softly, then brushed away the paper. "I
fell asleep."

"You're working too hard."

She shook her head and smiled lazily, looking a little

silly. She worked so hard at being efficient and competent it tickled him to see her foggy and foolish.

"You need sleep," he said. "Even business geniuses go to bed every night."

Fuzzy, she merely nodded and stood, then tipped to the side. He helped her upright and guided her forward. She let him walk her into her room, where she fell into the bed, burrowing into the pillow. This bed was much bigger and softer than the one in the guest room. He had the overwhelming urge to join her, hold that firm little body against him and make love to her.

Get a grip, Renner. She'd completely freak at the suggestion. And even if he did talk her into it, she'd probably tense up into a knot of performance anxiety and not enjoy a minute of it. He'd have to work his way off her to-do list—maybe get some work done on the cottage. He'd like to smooth the way for Penny to come out for a visit, too.

THE NEXT DAY, Ariel woke to her alarm, then heard the sound of rhythmic scraping and the blues. Jake was working. And early, too. That was good news. And she'd managed to sleep a full eight hours. More good news. She picked up the aroma of rich coffee. Mmm.

She showered and dressed and found Jake on a ladder scraping wallpaper off the living room, looking gorgeous, of course, in low-riding shorts, whistling along with B.B. King.

"Hi," she called up to him.

"Lox and bagels in the kitchen," he said. "There's more fruit, too. Hope you don't mind fixing it yourself.

Work, work, work." He indicated the tattered wall covering.

"Great job," she said, grinning. Things were definitely looking up.

Three hours later, Ariel hung up the phone from another of her former clients. A solid maybe. She'd detected weariness in the man's voice—*anything to get you off the phone*—but that was all right. It was a possibility.

She'd downloaded some hints on closing sales from the Internet and practiced a couple of calls in the mirror, and that had helped her. All she had to do was get her foot in the door. Then she'd be fine.

In between calls, she'd devised a promotional package using the quotes former clients had been happy to give her while she probed their future needs for her services. She was thorough. At least that. And now she had a *maybe*.

She felt a little better.

She looked up to watch Jake stretch high to scrape the stubborn wallpaper, admiring the taut muscles from fingertip to toe. Each ripple trailed down his body like electricity. Gawd, he looked good. If only he'd wear painter overalls so he wouldn't be so distracting.

Lucky lay under the ladder, earning all manner of bad luck, panting, sand outlining him like the chalk at a crime scene.

She'd had to ask Jake to turn down the music twice, but then he started whistling. She made him stop every time she made a call. The rest of the time, she tried to ignore the noise.

Footsteps thumped on the porch. Someone pounded

on the door. Jake turned at the sound—and caught Ariel still watching him. He grinned.

Hot with blush, she jerked her gaze away, then went to the door.

Two little boys and a twenty-something blonde stood with a mesh bag of sand toys on the porch. "Will you help us with a castle?" the woman called to Jake, barely glancing at Ariel in the doorway.

"How about it, Ariel?" Jake said, descending the ladder. "We could use a break, couldn't we?"

"Not me," she said, returning to her desk. "And you either. Don't you need to buy the paint and tile I picked out?"

"You promised," one of the boys said to Jake.

Jake looked at Ariel as plaintively as the kid was looking at him.

"Oh, go ahead," she said, irritated that he'd put her in the position of being the buzz kill.

"I'll meet you on the beach in a sec, guys," Jake said.

The boys hoorayed, the blonde smiled, and all three turned and headed down the steps.

Ariel shut the door and looked at him. "Why do I feel like the mean mom here?"

"Sorry. Don't worry about the painting. It'll get done."

"In my lifetime?"

"I won't let you down, Ariel."

"This is, what, the watched painter never paints?"

"Not bad. Good to hear a joke come out of you. You've been kind of intense on the phone."

"Intense?" Did she sound desperate?

"Maybe you should come with me."

"I can't." She sighed.

"Well, at least take your laptop and the phone onto the porch and get some fresh air."

"I'm all set right here."

"Think of it as a demo of the beach-office concept. If you hate it, fine." He grabbed her phone and the folder she'd been working on and headed for the kitchen door to the sunporch.

She groaned, but gave in, unplugging her computer and carrying it out to where Jake was brushing off two chairs with a paint rag. He gestured for her to sit on one. She did and he placed the other in front for her feet.

She put her laptop on her knees.

"Voila! Beachside office," he said.

"Thanks," she said, then glanced at the pile of ripped screen.

"I'll take care of that." He gathered up the pile and carried it down the stairs to plop near the trash barrel. When he returned he paused to admire her sitting on the porch. "See. Just because you're working, doesn't mean you can't be comfortable."

"I suppose not," she said.

"We'll be right over there if you change your mind," he said, pointing to where the two kids and the blonde had begun to dig in the sand.

"Fine," she said. "Thank you." She watched him jog off, then took a deep breath. The sea breeze held barely a hint of dead fish and the sun warmed her shoulders like a heating pad. The light had that salt-chiseled glimmer about it and there was a soft moisture in the air. The waves surged hypnotically in the distance.

Not bad.

Except now she had the urge to shut down her computer, turn off the phone and join Jake and his sand-castle gang, who were working away at the water's edge. Jake was scooping buckets of sand from between his legs like a dog digging a hole, and the boys were busy filling plastic molds of turrets and towers with the sand Jake tossed their way, laughing and calling out eager instructions. The woman leaned close, flirting with Jake, who seemed to be ignoring her.

Ariel had the urge to run out there and join in. What would an hour hurt? No. She might never get back to work.

She squinted at her computer screen—the sun's glare made it difficult to read. She turned her body away from the light—and the temptation of the beach fun—and determinedly set to work.

Twenty minutes later, she hung up the phone, her heart light with joy. She had a real, honest-to-goodness lead. Bob Small, a man who wanted to parlay his hobby of making custom car-seat covers into a business, had been referred to her by Trudy's accountant. They'd had a great conversation and made an appointment to meet in a week. Hooray! Things were happening. She scampered inside for the reference material she needed. As soon as she'd made a few notes, she'd join Jake's beach brigade for a fun break. She'd earned it.

A half hour later, she headed outside, ready to throw on an addition to the castle, maybe something for the serfs to live in.... Except everyone was gone. They'd built a fabulous castle, with long, high walls, perfect turrets, even a moat, then abandoned it. She saw Jake and his crew down the beach tossing a Frisbee, Lucky running between them. Laughter came to her on the breeze, children and adults mingling, melodic and carefree.

Of course they would include her in the game, but she was terrible at Frisbee. Nope, the moment was past. She sighed, transfixed by the way the sun gleamed in the sand of the castle. It looked so perfect and permanent, yet one wave and it would be gone. The group had worked like mad, then wandered off, content to have it destroyed by the tide.

Jake was right about the sea and its metaphors. This sand castle said something about wasted effort or the fragility of beauty or the fact that if you worked too hard you missed out on the fun. A little tidbit she would not share with Jake. He'd say *I told you so* for sure. She hated when he was right.

She would call her mother, though, since she had good news to report—and confirm their plans for the weekend visit. Having fun now and then would be good for both of them.

ARIEL WATCHED the willowy blonde in the tiger-striped bikini swipe a brush of paint across Jake's back.

"Hey," he said, swinging around to grab the girl around the waist, stealing her brush and holding it as if to paint her.

"No, stop," she said.

He dabbed a dot on her nose and released her.

Ariel wanted to throttle the woman. How much more obvious could she be, pretending to help Jake so she could flaunt her nearly nude, perfect body? And Jake seemed to enjoy every inch of bare skin, she noticed grumpily. And neither one of them was putting any of the lovely eggshell paint Ariel had so carefully selected on the walls, either.

It had been five days and Jake was still working on the living room. He had finished the roof repair, but he'd only looked at the electrical system and the bathroom lights kept shorting out. Every time she turned around, he was off the job—helping someone with a bike or a surfboard, teaching someone to surf or sail or dive, or stopping for a beer with some buddies.

Not to mention the fact that he sometimes forgot to answer the phone with, "Business Advantage," as she'd made him promise. He had a cell phone for personal calls, but he still got an occasional call on the land line. He'd missed giving her two important messages.

Any luck on a place to stay? she asked each day, but he'd say *almost* or change the subject or make something delicious—an eggplant parmesan to die for or a tofu salad with a dressing that made her moan embarrassingly.

The man was making her crazy. He was so there. Like a force of nature. And so attractive. Every time she tried to pop into the bathroom, he seemed to be nearby. The worst was once when they were both squeezed into the small space. She'd needed to blow her hair dry and Jake had insisted she could do it while he was shaving, barely clothed. They bumped elbows and hips angling for space and a view of the mirror. Then the power went off.

In the charged seconds while they grabbed for the door handle, they'd ended up in each other's arms. Jake seemed quite willing to hold on. She came away with a deliciously Jake-smelling blob of shaving cream on her nose and the memory of his arms around her—almost as vivid as that kiss in the ocean.

After that she'd vowed to stay clear of the bathroom when he was in it—and demanded he make the electrical problem a priority fix.

Now she watched him play around with the chickie instead of paint the living room, which she'd insisted he do right away, too, so her office would be clear of mess. It was a damn good thing Trudy wasn't paying him by the hour with Trixie—or was it Bambi? The girls and their bimbo names blurred—distracting him so effectively from his work.

Watching, Ariel felt an odd heat—and the urge to shove the girl off the ladder she'd obviously climbed to give Jake a shot of her legs and derriere.

"You missed a spot...to the left and up," Ariel called to Trixie-Bambi, who turned her way.

"Huh?"

Ariel pointed.

Trixie swiped at the place and missed it completely.

"I'll get it," Jake said and joined her on the ladder.

Ariel released a disgusted sigh. The sound drew Jake's gaze. "Room for one more," he said, patting the step.

"I have work to do," she said. *Unlike some people.*

"Your loss," Jake said and winked.

She turned away and studied her notes on a Request For Proposal she was working on. Why did Jake have so much fun all the time? Trixie or Bambi or Candi yelped at whatever Jake was doing to her waist.

"Could we lower the volume?" Ariel asked.

"Somebody took her grumpy pill this morning," Jake said.

"I just hope most of that paint makes it onto the

walls," she said, hating that she sounded like a spoil-sport.

After a while, Trixie got bored with painting and toddled off on her spiky sandals.

Jake climbed down and pulled up a chair, turned backward, close to Ariel. "You pissed?"

"How much are you paying your little helper? I hope not union scale."

"Hmm. Sounds like you're jealous."

"Jealous? How could I be jealous of a girl named Tiffany who pretends to paint so she can waggle her attributes for you?" *Of course, I'm jealous.* A little. She was only human.

"Now, now. Trixie *is* a painter. An oil painter. From Laguna."

"I'm impressed. Beautiful *and* talented." Now she truly was jealous.

"So are you. Beautiful and talented."

She ignored the kiss-up compliment. "One of your little chickies left her false eyelashes in the bathroom. I thought it was a spider and smashed it. Maybe mention it to her. If she's even noticed it's missing."

He shrugged. "You could play, too, you know. You make life too hard."

"And you make it too easy."

"If you'd lighten up a little, your work would go better."

She sighed. He did have a point. She remembered the sand castle she'd missed out on. The truth was she was more jealous of Jake than his girls—jealous of the way he'd arranged things so he got by without working very hard—and always on his terms. She wouldn't change her life, but something about the way he lived tugged at her.

"Have you seen my keys, by the way?" he said, standing.

"They're where they belong. On the key hook."

"The key hook?"

She pointed at the brass prongs she'd screwed into the wall beside the kitchen door where she put her own keys, the spare garage door opener that Jake kept mislaying, and Jake's keys when she found them under the couch, in the kitchen or on the bathroom sink.

"A key hook...what's next?" Jake muttered, going to the rack. "How about the receipt for the bike parts I bought? You got a hook for that?"

"Close." She handed him the folder she'd made for him. "I found the receipt crumpled into the sack."

"That's where I meant it to be," Jake said, looking through the folder.

"That's odd, since you threw the sack away."

"Oh, well.... What's this?" He held up the calendar she'd customized for him.

"So you can record your classes. I heard you rescheduling some because of the overlap."

"Oh." He looked over what she'd done and seemed impressed. "I guess I could use this."

"And you could put receipts and such in the folder."

"Maybe. But from now on, I'll handle my receipts, sacks and keys, all right?"

"I was just helping. Organization is one of my skills."

"You mean obsessions." He was grinning, so she couldn't quite take offense. He started out the door.

"What about the living room?" she asked.

"I've gotta pick up a few things. I'll get back to it. Check out those wallpaper border pattern books."

"I can't afford wallpaper border."

"Just look at the pages I marked," he said and he was gone.

She sighed in frustration, but on her next break she flipped through the books and liked exactly the ones he'd marked.

"I'M LOOKING FOR Ariel Adams?"

Jake looked down from the ladder where he was painting the cottage eaves at the short man standing on the porch. "She's not here right now," he said. She'd left without saying where, but he thought she'd had a client meeting this afternoon.

"We have an appointment at two," the man said, frowning. He was middle-aged and wore a faded T-shirt and a gimme cap, and had a cigarette pack sticking out of his T-shirt pocket.

"An appointment, huh?" Jake wiped the paint from his hands, descended the ladder, and opened the door for the guy. It wasn't like Ariel to be late, and he thought she planned to meet people at their offices until the cottage looked "decent."

"She must have gotten caught in traffic," he said. If he'd known she was meeting a client, he'd have cleaned up a little. He led the guy inside, then quickly turned down the music he had at max volume so he could hear it from the porch. "How 'bout I get you a beer while you wait?"

"Sounds fine," the man said, following him into the kitchen.

Jake introduced himself to the guy—Bob Small was his name—and asked him about his business so he wouldn't get pissed at Ariel for being late. The guy made custom car-seat covers, it turned out, and had some quandaries. Jake just let him ponder for a while. They started on a second beer. *Where the hell was Ariel?*

To be helpful, Jake told the story of his buddy with the custom surfboard shop. The money stuff took the fun out of it and the guy just gave up making boards. He figured that would help Ariel, because that way Bob would see the need for a business expert like her. Bob soaked up the story like a sponge.

To be sure the guy wouldn't leave, Jake made guacamole, broke out the chips and handed Bob beer number three.

Finally, Jake heard the garage door grind below them. "That's Ariel," he said. "Must have been some traffic jam. She's scrupulous about her schedule."

Bob Small just belched and asked him how much he paid for a twelve-pack of Tecate.

Ariel bustled into the house, caught sight of the guest and stood stock-still.

"This is Bob Small," Jake said, standing up. "I told him you must have been stuck in traffic."

"Bob! We had an appointment at your shop. It was locked...."

"I thought we were meeting here," Bob said, a goofy grin on his face. Jake slid the third beer out of the guy's reach.

"I guess I misunderstood," Ariel said. She flushed bright red and Jake felt bad for her. "I'm sorry you've had to wait so long. Come into my office—such as it is—and we'll get to work on your business plan."

"Actually, Jake here's helped me out," Bob said, looking a little sheepish.

"He has?" she said, her flush fading to pale.

"I just listened," Jake said, getting a bad feeling.

"Don't be so modest," Bob said, putting a hand on his shoulder. "Your buddy's situation is just what I don't want." He turned to Ariel. "I think I had the cart before the horse here on this growth idea. I'm plenty busy with word-of-mouth customers. Slaving all day to meet overhead is not what I want. I think I'll stand pat for now."

Ariel's face went even paler, except for two bright spots of red high on her cheeks. Uh-oh. "That may be true, but we could go over the possibilities in more depth than I'm sure Jake did." She shot him a glare, sharp and cold as an ice dagger.

"Thanks all the same," Bob said. He patted his pockets, looking for something, then pulled out a checkbook. "How about I pay you for the time?" Then he grinned. "Or maybe I should pay your assistant here." He jabbed Jake in the gut with an elbow.

"Just a little talk," Jake said, feeling like a heel.

"There's no charge, Bob," Ariel said softly. "I missed our appointment, and you appear not to need my services right now." She flashed Jake a pointed look. "Keep me in mind, though, if you decide to move ahead.... And if any of your friends need assistance, please give them my card." She pulled several from her purse and thrust them at him.

"You bet," he said, stuffing the cards into his front jeans pocket, where they'd undoubtedly get washed into mush. "Thanks again, Jake." He gave Jake's hand a hearty shake, looking at him like they'd just become poker pals.

Ariel walked her ex-client to the door, then turned on Jake. "What the hell did you think you were doing?"

"I had to keep the guy busy until you got here," Jake said, feeling sheepish. "I mentioned the surfboard shop just so he'd know he needed you. But he's not ready. You'd have figured that out eventually. I just saved you time."

"Right. You saved me time."

"I was afraid the guy would skate on you."

"He did, thank you very much." She blew out a breath. "It's just...unfortunate."

"Let me get you some tea." He headed for the kitchen, hoping to cheer her up, pleased when she followed him. He took the pitcher from the refrigerator and poured her a glass. "Gingko biloba—you look depleted."

"Depleted? I'm devastated," she said, taking the glass from him with shaking fingers.

"Come on, it's not the end of the world."

"It is for me," she said. Was that the shine of tears?

"There will be plenty of other clients," Jake said, hoping there would be. She looked so sad. He motioned for her to drink.

She did. "There has to be," she said, looking up at him, her green eyes cloudy with misery. "I have two months' savings and that's it. Once that's gone, I'll have to get a job somewhere—rolling burritos at the Del Taco, for all I know."

"You've made tons of calls. Something will come through."

"Nothing so far. Lots of *maybe*s and *in a year or two*s and *we'll keep you in mind*s, but no clients. Bob Small was it."

"Well, hell, I can get you a client." Brice was always bragging about expanding. He'd talk Brice into hiring her. He had to do something. Ariel looked so deflated...all her energy just *phhht*, like a bright balloon abruptly freed of air.

"Right. What? One of your surfboard buddies?" She looked at him with raw doubt.

"Exactly," he said.

She seemed to be fighting some retort, but gave up in despair. Where was that upthrust chin and locked jaw he knew so well? He hated seeing her like this and he'd helped make her that way.

She snatched her pillowy lip between her teeth and began the usual gnawfest. "I'll be all right. Losing Bob Small was a blow, that's all. I'm meeting with someone from a community college about teaching an evening class. And I have a networking luncheon tomorrow."

He thought about her admonition to herself—*Don't let fear rule. Keep on keeping on.* He was about to repeat it to her when he realized she'd be embarrassed that he knew her secret mantra. She seemed to gather herself, squared her shoulders and lifted her chin.

His heart swelled with relief and he vowed he'd get her a client if it killed him—or, rather, Brice, who was a notorious cheapskate.

JAKE PUSHED OPEN THE DOOR to Water Gear, clanging the bell. He breathed deep the great rubber, plastic, saltwater, mildew scent of the place and felt at home all over again. But today he had no time to shoot the breeze or check out new equipment. He was on a mission.

"What happened to you?" Brice said, reading his expression. "One of your honeys turn up pregnant?"

"God, no," he said. "I need to talk to you."

"I got no spare cash," he said, "and you know I don't loan money to friends."

"Hell, you don't loan money to anybody." The guy was so tight he reused paper cups until they dissolved. It had taken Jake years to get Brice to pay him close to what he was worth for the lessons and charter gigs Brice hired him for. Even now, the scheduling got to be a pain. Not to mention the lapses in income. "You want to expand this place, right?"

"Expand? I got my hands full with one shop. And my numb-nuts weekend guy over-ordered replacement shorty suits."

"But you said yourself what a great concept this is. You could take it to San Diego, even Mexico, remember? That's what you told us the other night."

"Before or after the second pitcher of margs?"

"Come on. *En vino veritas.*"

"Now with the Latin? I know I'm in trouble when you start showin' off your college ed-ju-cashun."

"The point is that I know just the person you need to talk to. My landlord."

"The brunette with the pointy name?"

"Ariel, right. She's a business consultant. She's good—got great ideas—and she's just getting started, so I'm sure you can score a great rate. She's big on planning—short-range, long-range, strategic, you name it, she plans it."

"Hold it. I've got to sit down for this." Brice lowered himself to the rickety stool by the cash register, pretending he'd become faint. "I don't believe it." He shook his head in exaggerated wonder. "Jake Renner, ape-shit over a woman."

To his chagrin, Jake felt himself heat. "It's not like that. I sort of caused her to lose a client, so I want to make up for it—and help you at the same time."

Brice pretended to cough and wave away smoke. "It's gettin' thick in here," he said. "Not to mention the fact I'm ankle deep in something foul."

"Come on, Brice. You could flounder around for years, spouting off about expanding, and never get off your ass and do it. She'll help you figure out what you want—cut to the chase."

"Look, I'm always glad to help you, pal. If you want to take out a boat to impress a woman, fine...or buy equipment wholesale on my account, fine. But this is my life here." He indicated the rack of snorkels, posters of various fish, photos of boats and, beyond, the rows of oxygen tanks and wetsuits. "I'm fifty years old. I'm not screwin' with my life just to help you get into some sweet thing's thong."

"It's not like that," he said. "Look, hire her, and if you don't think she's worth it...I'll pay her fee myself." Now that was a leap of faith on his part—one he wasn't so sure he should have taken. Not with the Penny fund hanging in the balance. But he had to do something to wipe out Ariel's despair. He'd thought she was a jittery overachiever. He'd had no idea she was so close to the edge.

Brice still looked suspicious. He'd have to give him

something more believable. "Okay. Here's the deal. She wants to kick me out of her house. If I get her a client, I can stay."

"I knew it," Brice said with a self-satisfied chuckle. "You dog. You never change."

A ripple of annoyance shot through him. Why couldn't he be doing something just to be kind? Didn't Brice know him better than that? They spent enough time together—sailing, diving, playing poker, hanging out. Of course they rarely talked about the deep stuff. Now and then Brice brought up his old girlfriend—and legendary heartbreak—from when he was Jake's age, but only when he was shit-faced. Still, Brice should know he was a decent guy.

"At least let me bring her out on the boat so you can meet her. She needs to relax and she can get a feel for your business."

"She needs to relax? I would have thought you'd have handled *that* by now."

"I have to live with her."

"Even more handy."

"Too complicated."

Silence.

"She's not my type," Jake added lamely.

Brice nodded slowly. "I get the picture."

"No, you don't." Though it was true that every time she started chewing on that puffy little lip he felt it in the groin. He wanted to kiss the poor thing better, get a hand on that tight rump, put a hitch in her breathing, a startle in her innocent green eyes. And there she was every night, lying in bed just a thin drop cloth away....

This rush of lust was due to the fact she was off-limits,

he was sure. Like being in an Italian restaurant on a low-carb diet—pure torture. "I want to give her scuba lessons—as an act of goodwill. You can take us for a dive and see what you think."

"Scuba lessons, huh? Whatever you say..." A smug look filled Brice's stubbly face. Okay, let him think that all Jake wanted with Ariel was a buddy-breathing session, as long as it got him what he really wanted—Brice wriggling on Ariel's hook. "I'll take you on a dive," Brice said, "but we leave my business out of the conversation, okay?"

Jake shrugged. Ariel would have to handle the man with kid gloves and what he'd seen of her sales technique told him she was more into clobbering clients over the head with a club and dragging them into her lair.

The distraction of learning to dive would help. Dipping into that alternate universe would jolt her out of her worries and fill her with wonder. He couldn't wait for that wide-eyed look new divers always got. On Ariel, it would be almost as good as delivering an orgasm. Hmm. His penis stirred. *Stand down*, he told himself, repeating his father's old command.

If Brice didn't work out for Ariel, he'd set her up with another of the business guys at the marina. It was the least he could do for a roommate.

7

"WHEN YOU'RE READY, Business Advantage will be there," Ariel said to her tenth not-interested-right-now cold call, two days after Jake had helped her lose Bob Small and his car-seat covers. She held her smile in place as she talked, but her heart was a boulder in her chest. She wouldn't convince anyone to hire her sounding like Eeyore. No more calls for today.

She still had leads from a friend from business school she'd run into at a networking luncheon. She would try those tomorrow when she was feeling more cheerful.

She picked up the piece of paper with the number of the temp agency. She should call and put her name in. It had been three weeks since she arrived and the stress was getting to her. She was even hopeful that Jake's beach buddy lead would come to something, though the likelihood was low.

She'd left another message for Trudy in the London office, but she'd been unavailable by phone. She needed advice from her mentor, an intervention or at least a pep talk.

Her mother was coming out to see the cottage on Saturday. Though she was looking forward to the visit, Ariel kind of regretted the invitation, knowing her mother would pick up her distress and worry about her.

She went to the kitchen to make tea. The place looked

like a war zone. Jake had ripped up the linoleum and the new tile she'd chosen hadn't come in yet. She'd complained about the chipped and rusty sink, so Jake had torn it out and hadn't connected with his buddy to get the new one, a leftover from a construction site.

She couldn't grouse since it was free, but now she had to make tea in the bathroom sink. She tamped down her annoyance. She could never quite get mad at Jake because he *was* working on the house like she wanted...just not the way she wanted.

Right now, he was off teaching a lesson, surfing some waves or helping a kid with a tree house. If only he'd move. *Working on it*, was all he'd ever say.

Of course, she could force him to move out. Demand it. Give him a deadline, then pack his stuff and set it on the porch, but she couldn't bring herself to do that. Even if he moved out, he'd still be here every day working.

She opened the refrigerator to find the cold chicken curry he'd put on a plate for her lunch, complete with peeled, sliced kiwi. If she kicked him out, he wouldn't fix her this great food.

In a way, it was a relief he wasn't here, even to restore her devastated kitchen, because of the ticking tension between them. The feeling built every day, flaring when she brushed against him in the hall or accidentally twined fingers accepting a mug of morning coffee from him, or slid into the coconut-scented steam of the bath as he moseyed out, a towel precariously balanced on his hips, a whistle on his lips. Sometimes, she feared she'd faint from the lust pouring through her blood in thick pulses.

Every night she lay on the other side of that drop cloth

listening for his breathing, hoping to hear the rustle of fabric as he burst through the barrier like Zorro to kiss her into surrender. Her ridiculous lust for him, on top of all the noise he made and the phone messages he flubbed and his constant interruptions and the mess he left in every room, was plenty of reason to want him out of her house.

But she didn't quite want that.

She wondered if he was as tempted by her as she was by him. Since the midnight swim, when she'd said no, he seemed to have given up the idea of sex with her, though she did catch a look now and then. Of course, he had plenty of other places to relieve those urges. Heather or Bambi or some other beach bunny. After the fuss she'd made about the bikini-clad artist, Jake had stopped bringing his playmates to the cottage, at least.

Ariel sighed, picked up the card with the temp agency number and started dialing.

She was interrupted by Lucky, who burst in the door Jake had left unlatched again. He trotted over to her and dropped a wet piece of driftwood on her lap. The stick stank of seaweed and streaked her skirt with sand and green slime. Great.

"Lucky...no," she protested weakly. "Wait for Jake."

But Lucky looked as desperate to play as she was to work.

She glanced at her computer screen with the frustrating list of failed leads, the temp agency number, then at Lucky's big brown eyes and the way his body quivered, anticipating every twitch of her muscles, every nuance of intention on her face.

What the hell? She could give up her dream just as

easily in fifteen minutes as right now. "Just a few tosses," she said, standing. Lucky yelped ecstatically and galloped for the door. Turning to be sure she was coming, he conked his head on the doorjamb. The poor dog couldn't believe his good fortune.

At the bottom of the porch steps, Ariel slid off her shoes and ran gingerly on tiptoe to the edge of the water where Lucky waited, prancing in place. The sun was pleasant, the air bright, the breeze light. Just being out here made her feel somehow less burdened. Maybe Jake was right about taking time for herself. Maybe having fun did make work go better. Hmm. She'd give herself one more day before she called that blasted temp agency.

She tossed the stick as hard as she could, watching it make a satisfying arc across the pale blue sky. Lucky lunged, hind legs churning like a greyhound after the rabbit. Such passion. She laughed. This *was* fun. And good for her. Good for Lucky, too, who trotted back with the stick and proudly dropped it at her feet. She threw it again in the other direction.

He brought it back.

She threw it again. He brought it back. She did it again. And again.

"Just once more," she'd said for the tenth time—she should get back to work—when Lucky gave a sharp bark and kept running past the stick. Toward Jake, she saw, who was heading her way, grinning. Such a great grin—big and intimate and just for her. Her heart warmed. Here she was playing catch with a dog on the beach while a handsome man came toward her, looking at her like she was all he wanted to see. *Life is good.*

When Jake got close, he gave her a thumbs-up.

"What?" she said, letting the stick dangle in her hand, while Lucky nudged at her thigh.

"I've just about got you a client," Jake said.

"You're kidding," she said, flinging the stick far over her head, her heart flying with it, light with hope.

"He's not in the bag yet. He owns a water sports equipment shop and a couple of charter boats. He kind of wants to expand."

"Kind of wants to? Like Bob Small?" She couldn't bear another false lead.

"Not like Bob. He's not big on change and he's a cheapskate, but if you don't come on like gangbusters, you can talk him into what I know he wants."

"You think so?"

"As long as you take it slow."

"Tell me about his business," she said. "Tell me everything."

Jake laid out the basics and she listened closely, her mind racing with possibilities, absently tossing the stick for Lucky whenever he nudged her with it. When Jake finished, she wanted to thank him. Her heart was so full the words were hard. "Thanks, Jake. This means more than I can say."

"It's the least I could do after the car-seat fiasco." The setting sun had turned Jake into a bronze god, his hair burnished, his skin glowing.

The waves lapped gently at Ariel's feet, sucking the sand under her toes, as if to pull the ground out from under her altogether. She wanted to show how she felt. It didn't feel right to hug him, but she moved forward, her arms slightly outstretched...

And Jake made the decision for her, pulling her into a hug that felt so good. This was okay, right? Just a friendly hug?

Except this was no loose, cheery roommate hug. This was a breast-crushing, erection-pressing, body-to-body embrace. And Ariel wanted to just melt into it, breathe in Jake's coconut and musk, let him kiss her, let something happen, fall into it, let go.... Her fingers dug into his back.

"It'll work out fine," he said into her hair. He was reading her mind.

She nodded into his neck. If it felt this good, maybe it would be fine....

"We'll go for a dive on his boat next week," Jake said, "so we'll start scuba lessons tomorrow."

"Scuba lessons?" Ariel's drifting lids flipped open and she pushed out of Jake's arms.

"Brice will warm up to you if you're interested in diving."

"You expect me to learn to dive? No way am I going underwater and breathing out of a bottle. It's bad enough thinking about all those creatures when you're at the surface, but actually seeing them face-to-face..."

"You'll love it, Ariel. It's not as scary as it sounds and I'll be with you every step of the way."

"Uh-uh. I can't." She crossed her arms and backed up, bumping into Lucky and barely catching her balance.

"If you want Brice as a client, this is the best way. We'll start slow. Take it step by step."

She did need a client. Badly. And this was the only prospect in sight. She chewed her lip. "I'll think about it."

THAT NIGHT JAKE COULDN'T SLEEP. He'd stayed out late, hanging at his favorite bar, nursing a slow brew, but he couldn't stop thinking about holding Ariel in his arms that afternoon. He'd even thought about bringing a woman home just to distract himself, but all he could think of was Ariel.

She'd felt so good—firm flesh, her curves melting into his body as though she was made to be in his arms. When she'd let go like that, he'd felt he'd really won something. Her trust, her lust, he didn't care which. It was like winning first place in some impossible competition.

He tossed and turned, shoved off the sheet, so the air would cool his chafed and burning skin. In the silence he could hear the ocean, its soft shushing usually his lullaby—not that he ever struggled for sleep.

Except tonight. He listened for Ariel. Did her breathing sound unsteady or was that just wishful thinking? He heard a sleepy moan. Then another—this one utterly hungry. She was having a sex dream.

His penis tightened, eager for action. *Down boy*.

Ariel murmured a word. Was it his name? He'd swear it was, and she'd said it with a needy edge that meant, *Help me, touch me, make it all better*.

No problemo. He was out of the bed in an instant. Two soundless strides and he was at the canvas cloth, listening hard, holding his breath. He heard the rustle of sheets, then nothing. Had she gone deeper into sleep or was she just waiting for him, hoping he'd push through the barrier and touch her where she ached. He longed to do that, to kiss her, soothe her while she bucked against his hand, moaning with pleasure.

Then he would push into her...slowly...still touching her, fighting his own orgasm long enough to enjoy her tight body, firm breasts, buttery skin. He pressed his hand flat against the canvas cloth. Should he go for it?

ARIEL WOKE to find herself clutching a pillow between her knees, her hips sliding forward, rubbing herself against the fabric. Another sex dream. And now she tingled with arousal. If only she'd stayed asleep long enough to climax. Except it never worked that way. She always got close and then woke up or drifted into mild frustration, then deeper sleep.

She sighed. That hug on the beach had felt so good. She kept reliving it, wanting more. She'd been lonelier than she'd realized. If only she could have a time-out from her life to explore Jake's arms and hands and mouth. She'd felt the hunger in him, too.

Why couldn't they do it? Relieve the tension, get it over with? She was prickly and achy, desperate to rub herself on something, like a cat in heat. Hell, it was just biology. She pushed herself out of bed and padded to the cloth curtain between her and the object of her lust. All she had to do was pull the cloth aside. She held her breath and listened. He was probably asleep. She could whip off her nightgown and slide between the sheets. They wouldn't even speak. It would be like a dream, not even real.

Then she heard an intake of breath—just inches away! Jake was standing on the other side of the cloth, wanting what she wanted. Oh, no. She backed up, electrified by the risk. She wasn't ready. Or maybe she was too ready.

Bad idea. She had to keep her focus, concentrate on her work.

Back in bed, she stared at the canvas, willing Jake to sweep it away, yank it down, set it on fire, anything.

Nothing.

Ariel rolled away from the curtain. First thing tomorrow, she would ask Jake to replace the drop cloth with a solid wall.

ARIEL DECIDED that what she needed to keep her focus— while fighting her fear of diving and her lust for Jake— was a good goal visualization session. So she headed to a building in Thousand Oaks with offices for lease right where she wanted to end up. The leasing agent happily walked her through the available suites, leaving her alone in one of the nicer ones while he took a phone call. She sat in a metal chair and pictured herself working here. She envisioned a client stopping by to praise her for saving his company, another offering to double her retainer, a third vowing to promote her at his business club meeting.

This could happen. It *would* happen. As long as she stayed focused. She'd do whatever it took to get here— even learn to scuba dive. Her stomach clutched. In the end, she'd agreed to let Jake teach her to dive.

Step by step, Jake had said. Step by step to a watery grave. She was either extremely brave or completely insane, and she wouldn't know which until she was a hundred feet under thousands of pounds of ocean, trusting her life to some puny mouthpiece and a tank of air on her back. And Jake.

She shuddered, full of fear. Maybe another visualization, since she was already in Thousand Oaks. She headed for the housing development where she hoped one day to live with the man who would meet her husband criteria.

She parked beside an especially perfect house, stared at the picture window in the red-brick front and conjured up her future Mr. Wonderful and their golden retriever. *Well, my darling,* he would say, *you've worked so hard to achieve your goals. I'm so proud of you.* Then he would lean down from his six feet, his dark eyes gleaming with desire for her...except, wait...his eyes had gone smoky-blue and he was only slightly taller than she. God, it was Jake looking at her with mischief. *Tag, you're it,* he said and shot her with a squirt gun before he ran off with...not her elegant golden retriever, but that goofy furball Lucky.

Stop it. Her husband would not be a lazy beach bum, but a dedicated professional and loving mate, who understood and valued her own ambitious nature. *Concentrate.* She squeezed her eyes shut, clenched her fists and called up the familiar image of her future husband. He was wispy, a little faint maybe, but there he was—tall, with dark, wavy hair. *Here's a rose from our garden,* he'd say and hand it to her. *Not quite as beautiful as you.* That was more like it. *Time to swim our laps,* he'd say, his guiding hand warm on her back. *But first, let's try on this scuba tank.* Jake again!

She banged her steering wheel. She was so upset, she couldn't even manage a decent fantasy in her dream neighborhood. Disgusted with herself, she headed home for her, gulp, diving lesson.

ARIEL SAT beside Jake in his Beetle as they drove to the marina for the dive trip, her stomach in a knot, her breathing shallow and shaky. It had been all well and good in the pool, where Jake had shown her how to use fins, a snorkel, the buoyancy-compensation vest and a mouthpiece. But now she would be in the deep, remorseless ocean.

She glanced at Jake as he pulled into a spot at the marina. He was whistling, completely calm. It was all his fault. Him and his coaxing smoky-blue eyes, his infectious smile and breezy confidence.

He glanced at her. "You'll do fine," he said, squeezing her knee. "Just let Brice do most of the talking. You'll learn what you need to know. The man loves an audience."

"That's not what I'm worried about," she said.

"What? You're scared about the dive? That's the easy part." He gave her a Cheshire cat grin. She half suspected he'd insisted on the dive to give her something life-threatening to distract her from obsessing about getting the client.

He had a point, of course. She'd changed her clothes three times and printed out two versions of "first thoughts" for Brice, which Jake had convinced her she should save until after the first meeting. Then he'd refused to let her bring her laptop along. "You start clicking on computer keys and Brice will think you're too high-end for him."

So, here she was, wearing light pants and a white cotton blouse over her swimsuit, carrying just a bag with a towel and a notepad, her pulse jumpy, glancing at Jake, who guided her by her elbow, his warm hand a comfort to her.

She did feel safe with Jake—odd because he was the last person she'd think of to count on. He couldn't even stay with a painting task for more than an hour. But he'd been a patient and masterful teacher, focused completely on her, demonstrating each technique with care, then helping her try each one again and again, until clearing her mask and snorkel and using the fins were second nature to her.

He'd stressed safety rules, showed her how to buddy-breathe. She did like that about scuba. Since you couldn't hear each other, you had to stay within sight of your buddy, checking eyes, knowing hand signals for trouble or danger or fear.

If something went wrong with your breathing apparatus, your buddy would give you air through the second mouthpiece or by taking turns with his own. Underwater, your life was in your buddy's hands. And with Jake as a buddy, she felt quite safe.

They walked down the pier, and she spotted the faded sign for Water Gear. Inside the weather-worn front door stood a tall, leather-skinned man, early fifties, his hair a sun-bleached brown, wearing a denim shirt and a canvas hat.

"Brice Logan, meet Ariel Adams," Jake said.

"Nice to meet you, Brice," Ariel said. "I'm honored to have this opportunity to..." Jake caught her eye. *Take it easy. Don't push.* "...meet you," she finished. "Jake's told me a little about your business."

"Don't listen to this dreamer," Brice said. "You hear

him tell it, I should end up the McDonald's of scuba shops."

"All he's told me is that you love what you do," she said.

Jake smiled and gave her a soft nod. *Nice and easy.*

"This is the place," Brice said, giving the worn, gouged counter a loving rub. "We rent out the best gear—no cheap crap." He showed her the brands and various pieces of equipment, complained about his inventory and his part-time workers. She asked questions about seasonal shifts in his business, keeping it light and conversational, but taking rapid mental notes, not risking her pad yet. She wished she'd slipped a dictation tape recorder into her beach bag.

She felt that familiar excitement, that joy when she began to absorb a client's world, make it her own, take on his hopes and dreams and help him shape the future into something he wanted. She'd been so worried about capturing clients, she'd completely forgotten how much fun this was.

"Hate to cut this short," Jake said, glancing at his watch, "but we need to hit the dive spot before the water gets murky."

"Guess I've been talking your ear off," Brice said as they made their way to the boat.

"And I've enjoyed every minute," Ariel said.

Brice looked at her, his gaze piercing, taking her measure. She could feel his interest, his respect.

Then the engine roared, the boat dug into the water and they were off. *Here we go. This is it. Into the ocean, deep and blue and dangerous.* Ariel's heart began to pound. To distract herself from what lay ahead, she asked Brice more questions, gently probing his goals and interests. He was a hands-on guy, not good at delegation, so she'd suggest a slow expansion and only with trusted staff. She was itching to assess the market and do a force-field analysis on the risk factors.

She caught sight of Jake. He was driving the boat, but watching her, too, looking pleased with himself. Like someone who'd arranged a blind date that turned into true love.

They reached the dive spot and Jake killed the engine. Instantly, Ariel's heart leapt to her throat. This was it. Underwater dozens of feet. She swallowed hard, trying to force her heart back down into her chest.

Brice caught the look on her face. "Jake's the best there is," he said, patting her trembling knee. "You'll do fine."

Her scuba suit on, Ariel let Jake help her with her tank and buoyancy-compensation vest. She tried to keep her teeth from chattering in fear.

"It's just like in the pool, only magic," he said in her ear. "Just stay close and keep breathing."

"I'm not sure I can do that—keep breathing, I mean." She tried to smile.

Jake squeezed her shoulder. "You'll do fine. You're a natural."

Light glinted off the water, the gun-metal blue of the sea blending into the lighter color of the sky. The shore seemed miles and miles and miles away.

Jake went in first, holding his mask in place and falling backward into the water, as he'd taught her. She went in right after him, gasping at the cold shock of the water, until her body heat warmed the water between her suit and skin.

She released some air from her vest so she dropped a few feet below the surface and hung there, suspended.

Her breaths were quick and harsh and she realized she'd soon hyperventilate. She forced herself to slow her breathing and looked up at the surface, bright with sunlight. The bottom of the boat was a comforting shape above her. If only she were up there, safe and sound. Jake kicked over to her and held up an "okay" gesture as a question. She returned it. So far, so good.

He nodded, then pointed down. She looked and saw an unbelievable new world—a forest of swaying kelp, impossibly fragile-looking pink anemones, antlers of flowery blue coral, purple cabbage-like plants and craggy stone. Amazing.

So this was why people risked drowning and shark attack! A group of neon-gold fish, brilliant against the gray-green of the sea, swam past. Their bright beauty made her make a sound as close to a gasp as she could manage while gripping a mouthpiece between her teeth. She spotted a skittering lobster on the ocean floor—some forty feet below—and a spiky pincushion of a black urchin rolling past a thick-armed magenta starfish.

Ariel looked at Jake, amazed. He was watching her face, his expression like a parent at Christmas, absorbing his child's joy. He took her hand and squeezed through the glove. *I know. It's magic.* A look passed between them. Here they were in the soft, salty water, poised halfway between the ocean floor and its surface, deep in the wonder of a new universe.

She noticed Brice swimming nearby. He pointed at a piece of coral, where she could see a fat sea cucumber— bright yellow—waddle by. Then she spotted a moss-colored moray eel near a fan-like coral so yellow it practically glowed.

Jake pulled something out of his vest pocket and scattered it. Suddenly they were surrounded by dozens of fish in every shape, a few brightly-colored, most gray or green or silver, but shimmering, speckled and striped—some narrow silver flickers like minnows, others round and fat or broad and flat, some with odd beaked faces—and all of them whisking by, snapping at what Jake had released. Peas. She saw that now. She shrieked as a gray fish as big as her head darted straight for her then snapped at a pea mere inches from her face mask.

She looked at Jake and made out that he was laughing at her. She nodded her head violently, trying to show him how delighted she was, but she could tell he already knew. She whirled in wonder, watching the velvety fish as they snacked around her, their fins waving lazily, gills fluttering, eyes unblinking.

When the food had been eaten or had sunk, Jake took her hand and they began to kick through the water. A shot of air in her vest and she rose like a flying superhero to skim over the tops of little hills of coral and stone, past tall forests of swaying kelp, and then dipped lower to look more closely at the tiny colorful blossoms of sea plants, the antlered and fan-like coral, the tiny camouflaged, skittering animals and fish.

A bat ray swung lazily by, like a bird with slow wings, menacing and beautiful. She and Jake cruised along, wagging their fins lazily and she stared, eyes so wide they hurt, taking it all in, glancing at Jake, who gently showed her things she would have missed—an unusual starfish, an octopus hiding in a crevice, a crab scuttling drunkenly by—all underwater gifts he seemed to offer her.

She wished she had one of those waterproof slates so she could write exclamations to Jake. She tried to memorize everything she was seeing so she could mark them off on one of the laminated fish charts she'd seen in Brice's shop.

All too soon, Jake tapped at his watch, holding his wrist in front of her face. Time. They were running out of oxygen and had to ascend.

She nodded and he squeezed her hand, acknowledging her disappointment. She shifted so she was upright and they faced each other and slowly kicked upward. She counted, knowing they should take a minute for every ten feet they'd been below to allow the oxygen time to leave their bloodstream, but she knew Jake would never let harm come to her. He was her dive buddy. And her friend. A fact more wonderful than it should be.

JAKE WATCHED ARIEL break the surface. She dropped her mouthpiece, ripped her mask off and went nuts describing what she'd seen. He had to hold himself back to keep from hugging her and kissing her and bursting out laughing at her. Brice would never let him live that down, so he contented himself with agreeable remarks: "I saw that.... Yeah, far out.... Totally cool."

They climbed onto the boat and pulled off wetsuits and gear, Ariel chattering like a kid the whole time. "I can't believe this exists.... It's like another universe.... Forests and mountains and plains each with distinctive kinds of life."

Brice lit a cigar and watched her, nodding and grinning like a wizard. Brice loved this business. So did Jake, for that matter. He'd seen people go crazy before—knew more than one who'd quit his job and bought a boat so he could dive full-time—but watching Ariel succumb to the sea was something special. Something about her really got to him. Her intensity, he guessed. Her energy and drive. She made him feel alert. She made him think, reexamine things he'd taken for granted. The light in her face right now was pure pleasure.

On the other hand, he didn't appreciate the twinkling *aha* in Brice's eyes as he watched the two of them interact. So, maybe Jake had it going on for Ariel. What of it?

While Ariel got Brice to go over a color chart of the fish in the area so she could list the ones she'd seen, Jake went below and fixed a sand dab salad for the three of them.

They came down for Ariel's notebook, and he could hear that Brice was the one asking questions now, pondering the potential of Water Gear's expansion. The diving had relaxed Ariel and she sounded confident and competent. He grinned. He'd connected two friends and they'd both benefit. Not too bad for a day's work—and he'd gotten in a dive, too.

Interrupting the two, who were bent over a calculator, to get them to eat, Jake caught Brice's wink of approval. *The lady knows what she's doing.*

"I'm starving," Ariel said, surveying the plate of salad. "Salt water and terror must increase your appetite." She took a big bite. "Mmm, this is delicious, Jake." Ariel looked at him—the first look in a while—and he realized he'd missed her gaze.

"Glad you like it."

"Jake's good crew," Brice said. "He captains, he's a scuba master and he runs a great galley. A regular Jake of all trades."

"What are you after, Brice?" Jake said. "I'm not doing any more freebie lessons. And I need advance notice when it's a big group." Now and then he wished he could book his own lessons. It was better to leave the hassle to Brice, probably, but he could see some improvements Brice should make if he'd ever take advice from anyone.

"Nothing like that," Brice said. "I just want Ariel to know who she's dealing with here."

"I think I'm beginning to," she said softly.

Jake looked at her. Their gazes caught and held. Ariel stopped chewing. He felt that beat of tension, that pounding in his head. He wanted this woman. Her hair was slicked back, black as seal fur. The water had erased her makeup and her skin was flush with sun—in fact she had a little burn going. He should get sunscreen on her. She looked right on a boat. God, he wanted her.

"I said, pass the salad." Brice's words came faintly to him and he realized that wasn't the first time the man had made the request. He didn't remember ever wanting a woman so badly he missed hearing his own name.

Something was going on here. He reminded himself that Ariel wasn't the kind of woman who just had sex. She went into things for keeps. So why didn't that scare him?

8

"THAT WAS AN amazing, absolutely perfect day," Ariel said to Jake, looking up at him as they walked along the beach. They'd gone on a second dive, then returned to Water Gear so she and Brice could go over more details. Now they were walking along the beach. It was sunset and entirely too romantic, but Ariel was too happy to care. "I think I can really do something with Brice.... And the scuba...wow. It was heaven...really magical. That's probably cliché, but it's so true. I had no idea all that incredible life was under there. I thought it would be scary, but it was beautiful and natural. And...wow... just wow."

"Now you know."

"Yeah, now I know." She sighed, then took the fish chart Brice had given her from her beach bag. She'd marked off the creatures she'd seen with a wax pencil. "And I'm halfway through this chart."

"You're supposed to enjoy the experience, not collect it. Give me that." He took the chart away from her.

"That's how I remember things—by writing them down. Give it back."

"Remember it here," he said, tapping her forehead, "and here," softly touching her chest just above her cleavage. "In your heart."

"I do," she said softly. "It is in my heart." Their eyes

met. Jake had shown her the wonders underwater and
now he was grinning at her, happy that he'd made her
happy, and she felt so good being with him. "But I want
to record it, too. That's who I am." She reached to take
the card from his hand, their arms brushing. They were
practically dancing.

"Then come and get it." He darted away from her and
into the evening tide, kicking up sand as his toes dug
into the wet beach.

"You rat!" she said, dropping her bag and running after him. The wet sand was cold, but she hardly noticed.
Her internal heater was keeping her warm, burning
with the desire to be near Jake. She ran after him, heed-
less of everything but the man in her sights, so that she
didn't see the wave. When it hit she went down—
fwap—onto the sand, laughing. When the wave re-
ceded, she found Jake lying beside her.

"You okay?" he asked, leaning over her, braced on an
elbow, sand streaking his face.

"Fine," she said, aware that she'd just been assaulted
by all she hated about the beach, but she didn't mind
one bit. The delight of lying near Jake masked anything
unpleasant. "More than fine." She brushed the sand
from Jake's cheek, enjoying the firm muscle and solid
bone beneath her fingers. The retreating wave tugged
the sand from under her, making her feel unsteady, a little unsafe—a feeling that intensified as she looked up
into Jake's warm eyes, blue as the sky and the sea.

"Here." Jake handed her the fish chart, now wet and
sandy. "I haven't been such a bad roommate, have I?"
He pushed a strand of hair from her cheek.

"No. Except for the noise and the mess and the confusion—and not remembering to give me messages."

"Yeah, but what about the food?"

"The food's been great."

"You'll miss me when I'm gone."

She looked into his blue eyes. The sunset made them glint with gold. Water rushed under their bodies, further eroding the ground, tickling her, warning her, but she couldn't look away from Jake's face. "So don't," she said softly, looking at Jake, her visiting sea god, his eyes full of affection and promise in the dull-gold dusk light.

"Don't what?"

"Don't move out."

"I hoped you'd say that." And then his lips met hers and his arms convulsed around her from under the sand and the kiss was perfect—warmer and stronger and deeper than the first.

She knew this was a bad idea, but surely she could enjoy this kiss—the bookend to the fabulous day. A kiss to celebrate the excitement of diving and winning a client and the glory of this perfect man holding her. It was a *From Here to Eternity* moment, with the waves lapping romantically at them and Jake's mouth on hers, his fingers in her hair, turning her face so he could taste more of her, moving over her. She could have this moment, couldn't she?

Then the mother of all waves slammed down on them, churning everything, forcing sand into her eyes, water up her nose. She rolled to the side to escape and sand scraped her sunburned back like sandpaper on raw skin.

She coughed and choked, pushing up from the punishing sand. The pain put a sharp end to the dreamy moment she might have let drag on to a dangerous end. "That was bad," she said, coughing, salt stinging her eyes and burning inside her nose.

"Just a wave," he said, reaching for her.

"That's not what I mean," she said. "We can't do this."

"Sure we can. I can't stop wanting you. At night it's all I can do to keep from busting through that stupid curtain to grab you. Tell me you don't feel the same."

His words made her heart sing, but the sting of her back and the burn of saltwater in her nose kept her sane. "I do feel that way, but—"

"Then why fight it?"

"Because I'm different from you. I don't just jump into bed." She'd been tempted to lose herself in a man who was just a seashell's toss away from dozens of women he'd had *From Here to Eternity* moments with. And Ariel would not be just one more.

She pulled away from his hands and pushed herself to her feet. "I've got to go in. I'm sorry." She bent to get her fish chart and ran, stopping to nab her beach bag. When Jake didn't follow her she felt both relieved and disappointed.

She dashed into the bathroom, rinsed quickly in the shower, then grabbed a towel and lotion for her sunburn before she darted into her room to hide. She'd forgo her bedtime cleaning and brushing rituals tonight. She rubbed lotion gently onto her burned skin, then lay down on the bed, still sandy and very sad. She was naked—hadn't even put on her pink nightgown—and didn't want to think about why. She ached all over for Jake—a way worse pain than her sunburn.

She heard him enter the house and her whole body perked with anticipation. Would he toss away the drop cloth like he'd said he wanted to? He couldn't. Shouldn't. She wished desperately that flimsy barrier were an armor-plated wall. Something suitable for a nuclear plant. Impenetrable, unblastable. Safe. She remembered with dismay that she'd told him not to move out. That meant the only protection she had from Jake was their good sense and self-restraint. That should be enough. All the same, tomorrow she'd ask him to fix the wall.

JAKE STOOD in the living room and slowed his breathing. He could practically hear Ariel's heartbeat in the little house, sense her breath coming and going in harsh bursts. That wave hadn't doused the heat between them one bit.

And it was more than heat, Jake realized. Kissing her there in the surf, holding her in his arms had made him feel so happy...and so lost. Like a new surfer when the first wave slammed you into the sand, churning everything like a washing machine so you weren't sure which way was up for air.

What if he was in love with her? The idea had startled him, but when she broke away, he realized she was right. She was so different from him, so damn serious about every little thing. He wondered if she was wearing that pink monstrosity of a nightgown. Kind of sexy in a repressed virginal way....

Let it go. Move on. He could fall in love, all right, but it wouldn't last. And with a woman like Ariel love was way too risky. He couldn't bear to put pain in those wide and earnest eyes.

He knew how to let go. Spent his youth training for it, thanks to the Admiral. *Belay that, sailor*, he'd bark when Jake launched a last-ditch plea to stay with friends until the school year ended. *Load your duffel, son, we move out at o-nine hundred.*

Now, he valued that ability to pack light, stay on the balls of his feet. So it was good that Ariel was sensible. He'd keep helping her, though—take her diving again, maybe teach her to sailboard—and give her all the business leads he could. He'd just stay clear of the rest.

He forced himself to pick up the stack of mail on the table. A couple bills he could delay paying, some advertisements and an invitation to a reception at the marina. Hmm...

ARIEL WAS STILL STARING at the drop cloth when it whipped open and Jake stood there. He'd come after her. Her throat closed shut to keep her heart from jumping right out. She felt torn in two—half of her moaning *thank God*; the rest crying *No, God, no.*

"I have an idea," he said softly.

Me, too.

"A business guy I know is throwing a cocktail reception on his yacht," he continued.

What? She'd thought he'd come to make love to her and he was talking about a party? She shook her head, made out a white card he was tapping against his palm.

"It's a great chance for you to make business contacts," Jake said. "Lots of rich corporate types with boating habits. Will you come with me? It's Sunday after-noon."

She had to clear her throat to speak, even though her heart had flopped back down where it belonged in her chest. "Sure. That would be great. Thanks for thinking of me."

"I'm always thinking of you," he said softly.

"Oh." Her heart swelled. "Me, too. Of you, I mean."

"Do you think I should move out? Are things too...much...now?"

"No," she blurted, knowing she'd said that for all the wrong reasons. "We can handle this. We're adults." *Right.*

"If you're sure," he said.

"I'm sure," she lied.

"Okay, then. Get some sleep," he said, then he added more seriously than she'd ever heard him, "You're right about us. It would get complicated."

She only nodded. After that she lay awake, afraid she'd feel the impulse to go to Jake's bed. Before she could do anything stupid, though, she heard Jake bang-ing away at something at the other end of the house. He was working again. She had half a mind to join him, since she doubted she'd sleep a wink the rest of the night.

ARIEL DRAGGED HERSELF out of bed the next morning at seven, exhausted from barely sleeping, and staggered into the kitchen to find Jake whistling over a mug of cof-fee. How did he manage to survive so cheerfully on so little sleep? She saw that the kitchen sink was in place.

"You put in the sink," she said.

"I thought since your mother was coming I should get the kitchen in shape," he said.

"Thank you," she said, amazed that he'd remembered. He had such a *yeah, right, whatever* approach to the world, she was always surprised at how much attention he paid to things. The previous day's events had almost made her forget about her mother's visit.

"Bad night?" Jake asked.

She nodded and the movement seemed to make her brain slosh.

"Me, too," he said. They stood there, close together, neither seeming to know what to do with their hands or eyes.

"Sit," Jake said finally, pulling out a chair. "I'll get you coffee and food."

"Don't be so nice to me, Jake," she said shakily.

"I'm a saint, what can I say?" he said, putting down the steaming mug of what she could tell was a special mocha-cinnamon blend he'd been playing with.

She breathed in the steam, pulled in the glorious aroma and felt a little better. The microwave dinged and Jake pulled out a plate of frittata and placed it before her. It smelled great, but she couldn't take a bite. Her stomach was knotted tight and her appetite was shot.

"You have to keep your strength up if you plan on resisting me," he joked.

She managed a wan smile and took a bite.

"I'm taking off," Jake said. "I need the burnt umber you want for the bathroom and I have to check out some gear for Brice. I'll be back in time to meet your mother."

"You don't need to be here," she said, not sure she wanted her mother to pick up the vibe between them.

She was sure Deirdre Adams would not approve of Jake. And when she caught Ariel making moon eyes...she'd be so disappointed.

"Come on. I have to meet the woman who's more serious than you. See you. I'll bring back beer."

"My mother's not a big drinker."

"It's the beach, sweetheart. Salt air. Gotta have beer."

"Okay," she said, waving at him. Afterward, she realized how eerily domestic this had been. Jake had fixed the sink, prepared her breakfast, even told her his plans and promised to return to meet her mother—bearing refreshments, no less. Extremely appealing...and very confusing. Ariel put her head in her hands.

What would her mother think of the beach house? It was only moderately better than when Ariel'd arrived. The kitchen floor and sink were in, but color tests of yellow, cornflower and pumpkin were smeared like bad graffiti on the walls. The living room and her office were nearly normal—except for more bikes Jake intended to repair and one of his damnable surfboards. The wall between the bedrooms was still down, the outside of the cottage was half painted, and there were construction items, ladders and sawhorses scattered like glacial effluvia in the sand. So much for "getting it in writing," as her mother had suggested.

But Ariel did have her first client—Water Gear—and the Sunday reception would give her valuable contacts. That cheered her up and cleared her head. The amazing coffee helped, too.

Deciding to maximize the two hours before her mother arrived, Ariel dug into her plan for Brice, but she'd barely gotten started when someone banged on the door.

Three teenage girls stood on the front porch, tentative smiles on their faces. "Hi. Is, um, Jake home?" One said. Ariel recognized her as Jake's sister.

"Not at the moment. You must be Penny."

"He told you about me? That's great." She shot her friends an I-told-you-so. "And you're Ariel, right?"

"He told you about me?"

"Um, yeah." Penny blushed. What exactly had Jake said? Her own face warmed.

"So, we got a ride out here," Penny said, "and I, uh, wanted to show my friends Jake's place—your place, I mean—and see it for myself, since I haven't yet been out here and all...."

"I'm not sure when Jake will return...."

"Oh, gee..." Penny looked uncertainly at the other girls.

"Why don't you come in and wait," Ariel said. With work to do and her mother on the way, the last thing she needed was a crowd, but how could she turn the girls away? "Can I get you some iced tea or a soda?"

"How about daiquiris?" one of the girls said.

"Sheila!" Penny said with a frown of disapproval. Then she brightened. "Actually, I could make virgin ones. Jake showed me a great recipe. Do you mind?" she asked Ariel.

"No. That would be fine," she said, feeling gently rail-roaded.

"Terrific," Penny said and led the two girls inside. "This place looks great." Her gaze roamed the living room.

"It's getting there," Ariel said. "The kitchen's this way. You girls can make yourselves comfortable," she said to the other two girls, who were already heading for the stereo.

In the kitchen, Penny looked out the window on the kitchen door. "A sleeping porch...wow," she said. "We could have easily crashed here."

"Crashed?" Ariel asked her, standing with the blender in her hand.

"Jake said it would be too crowded. I was going to come out and spend the weekend a while back, but Jake nixed it when you showed up. We're staying somewhere else, though, so you don't have to worry about us or anything."

"Oh, good," she said, keeping the irony out of her voice. "What else do you need for these daiquiris?"

Penny rattled off the ingredients and the two of them were soon working elbow to elbow in the small kitchen. In the living room the girls had to shout at each other over the volume of the music they were playing.

Penny forgot the blender lid on the first batch, so Ariel took over while Penny wiped iced strawberry splotches off the cupboards and freshly tiled floor. Grrr.

"So, what do you think of Jake?" Penny asked her, sponging off Ariel's white clam-diggers. "Club soda should keep that from staining."

"I'll try that." *Lord.* "Jake is very...nice."

"And cute, too, don't you think?" Penny stood and dabbed at Ariel's blouse.

"He's good-looking. Sure. I'll handle that." She took away the cloth, which was having no effect on the pink stain, then bent to find a serving tray.

When she stood, Penny was looking at her intently. "I know he acts all easy and cool and whatever," she said, accepting the tray, "but he's really deep. You've noticed that, right?"

"I imagine so," Ariel said, excruciatingly uncomfortable at the way Penny's blue eyes dug in and poked around just the way Jake's always did, so she changed the subject. "What I have noticed is how fond he is of you."

"Fond! He's obsessed!" Penny clanged the tray onto the counter. "And bossy as hell."

Pleased to have diverted the girl, Ariel didn't even ask her not to swear. She just poured the frosty pink drinks into mason jars and set them on the tray.

"He's always telling me what to do," Penny continued. "Live your life, go out. Don't let the parents lock you in the tower. Blah-de-blah. He doesn't realize that I'm, like, an adult."

"That's a big brother for you."

"You mean Big Brother," she said, making finger quote marks, "as in black helicopters and listening bugs in the bathroom." She flounced off with her tray of virgin daiquiris.

Ariel smiled. She liked the girl, for all her pushiness. She was sweet and energetic and she clearly loved her brother.

After that, Ariel found herself making nachos and two kinds of dip while Penny mixed up some brownies. She felt like she'd been dropped into a surprise party—only the surprise was on the party host. She thought about all the work she had to do, then remembered the day she'd missed out on the sand castle. She'd just try to go with this, find the fun where it lay.

She'd put the nachos in the oven when the front door banged opened and a dog barked. "What the hell?" Jake's voice. And Lucky, no doubt. The girls squealed and exclaimed over the dog.

"Pen? What are you doing here?" Jake stood at the entrance to the kitchen.

Penny dropped the beater and ran to hug him. "We had a free weekend and since Cindy was in town, Sheila and me thought we'd just stop by."

"You could have called first. I'm sorry, Ariel," Jake said, surveying the mess in the kitchen. He reached up and wiped a blob of strawberry off the molding of one cupboard.

"It's fine," she said, almost believing it.

"What are you up to, Pen?" he said, shooting her a look.

"We're staying with Cindy's cousin. He goes to UCLA and he has an apartment."

"You're staying with a college guy. Unsupervised? Absolutely not."

"I know what I'm doing. You always say, 'go explore.'"

"Explore life and places, not horn dog college guys." Jake glared at her like a displeased parent. It was fun to see Mr. Laid-Back go all uptight.

Penny folded her arms stubbornly.

Ariel sighed. She knew how to fix this. "Why don't the girls stay here? They can sleep on the sunporch."

"Really?" Penny asked her. "You wouldn't mind?"

"No. Like you said, there's plenty of room."

"See. I told you she'd be cool about it," Penny said to Jake.

"You told her I would object?" Ariel said to Jake, who looked sheepish.

"Oh, yeah," Penny added. "He said you wanted to kick his ass out of here."

"Oh, really?" she said, shooting Jake a look.

"I didn't say that...exactly. Are you sure it's okay, Ariel? Because I can get the girls a hotel room...."

"No, no. It'll be fun to have them."

"And they won't be any trouble," he said, then turned to Penny. "Will you?"

"Absolutely not." Penny crossed her heart. "We'll be, like, quiet as mice."

There was another knock at the door. "Oh, Sheila invited a couple of guys for the beach part," Penny said quickly. They heard Sheila greet the new arrivals—boom-voiced young men.

"Penny..." Jake warned, but she'd rushed to the living room. "I'm sorry," he said to Ariel.

"It's really all right." She smiled, pleased to notice that it *was*. She was having fun, too. And hardly worrying at all. "Why don't you finish Penny's brownies? I'm doing nachos."

"Don't you have work to do?"

"Yes," she sighed, "but I'm trying to go with the tides this time—you know, your philosopher's ebb and flow?"

Jake chuckled softly. "Come here," he said and pulled her close. He wet a thumb and brushed it along her cheekbone. "Got some war paint," he said, looking into her eyes. It got easier and easier to slip into this intimacy with him.

She smelled something burning. Her nerves? No, corn chips. She rushed to open the oven. Black smoke billowed out and she used a towel to remove the tray of blackened cheese and chips, which she dumped into the trash.

While she scraped the tray clean, Jake grated more cheese. The kids in the other room yelled to each other over the music.

"God, they're loud," Jake said, shaking his head. "You sure you're okay with this?"

"I like Penny," Ariel said, setting the scraped tray where Jake could pour fresh chips onto it. "She goes for what she wants—in a nice way. She thinks you obsess about her, by the way."

"I look out for her," Jake corrected, sprinkling grated cheese onto the chips.

"But you don't realize she's, like, um, an adult," she said, imitating Penny.

"God." He grinned. "She's a trip, huh?"

"She does all right for herself. She finagled a weekend at the beach house despite your mean old roommate."

"Clever girl." His face looked serious then. "I don't want her to struggle and suffer because of what happened with me."

"She doesn't seem to be suffering." She sprinkled green chiles onto the chips, enjoying working with Jake in the smoke-misted kitchen, the smell of burnt corn reminding her of October popcorn and cozy fall nights.

"I'm making sure," he said, helping her with the chiles. He paused, then spoke, not looking at her, "I'm sending her on a trip to Europe—a study abroad program."

"Really?" She stopped sprinkling to look at him.

He glanced at her, then back down, as if he'd regretted the confession. "It's a surprise for after graduation. That's what this construction job is for—to fund the trip."

"What a nice thing to do," she said.

He shrugged like it was no big deal.

"It's unusual, though," she added.

"And if the Admiral gives her a bit of trouble about going, I'll be in his face." Jake slid the new batch of nachos into the oven and returned to the bowl of brownie batter.

"You're on bad terms with your father still?"

"We're polite to each other. He thinks I'm throwing my life away, and I think he's never lived his. I feel sorry for my mother, who's put up with his silences and moods and all the transfers over the years."

"She must love him."

"Yeah," he said, as if that were stupid. There was trouble here, she could see. *He acts all easy and cool and whatever, but he's really deep.* That's what Penny had said about him.

Jake was certainly more than a beach bum who lived only to play, as she'd originally concluded. He was devoted to his sister and she already knew he was a patient teacher. His construction work was excellent—when he did it. Maybe all that "whatever" stuff was an act. Maybe with someone special in his life he'd show his more stable, responsible side....

"Taste this," Jake said, holding out a spoon dripping

with chocolate, unaware of the swell of hope inside her. He was just going to feed her again, as he'd been doing since the day she'd arrived, a perfectly innocent gesture.

But this time it would mean more. Ariel gripped his wrist, pulled the spoon to her lips and slowly licked it, holding his gaze, her heart pounding, her pulse racing. *What am I doing?*

Jake's eyes flared.

"Mmm," she said, telling him she wanted more.

"Ariel," he whispered, then leaned in to kiss her. In the background she heard the phone ring, but she didn't care. Let the machine take it.

They'd barely brushed tongues when Penny shouted, "Ariel. Your mom's on the phone!"

Damn. Damn. Damnity damn.

She jerked away from Jake, who kept his eyes on her. *More later*, he was telling her.

She picked up the phone and realized her mother should be arriving, not calling.

"We'll have to reschedule, sweetie," her mother said, not even waiting for Ariel to say hello. "I just can't take today off. Myra's son has a martial arts test."

"But you need a break. We agreed."

Her mother chuckled. "I'm fine. Really."

"How can they make you work? You already booked the vacation day, right?"

"They're not making me. It turns out we need to order supplies. It's just better if I do it. It saves time."

"I'm so disappointed."

"How about if I come out next Sunday after my shift? I can bring dinner."

"I guess…." She felt hurt, but she understood. Her

mother had a strong sense of ownership about her work. She felt that way, too, but what was one day at the beach?

"I'm disappointed, too, sweetie," her mother said. "But enjoy the day anyway. You're right that we all need a break from time to time."

"Did you ever intend to actually come?" she asked gloomily.

"Of course I did. I even bought a swimsuit, a big sun hat, and some 60 SPF sunscreen in case we decided to brave the beach. Things just come up." Her mother sighed, but Ariel could tell she wasn't nearly as upset as she was trying to sound.

"Right, I guess."

A burst of raucous laughter from the living room drew Ariel's attention and she saw that two guys were wrestling dangerously close to her computer.

"*Hold it!*" She lunged into the room to block their tumble onto her desk. The shamefaced roughhousers retreated across the room.

"What was that about?" her mother said when she returned.

"Nothing. Jake's sister has some friends over."

"Jake? Your handyman?"

Handyman? "Uh, yes." Handyman, roommate, scuba buddy, business agent, obsession and sex god, but how could she explain that to her mother? She could hardly explain it to herself.

There was a shout and a clunk from the living room. Jake cringed. "I'll get them out of here," he whispered to her. "Come join us when you're done. I'll take the nachos, you bring the brownies when they're done. We'll be playing volleyball."

She nodded as he headed off.

"Sounds awfully noisy," her mother said.

"It can be," she admitted. "But you get used to it."

"So he's still working on the house?"

"Uh, yeah."

"I hope you're not paying him by the hour."

"Trudy's paying him a flat rate. Today's not really a work day...."

"He's still living with you, isn't he?"

"For a good reason," she said quickly. "He's saving money so he can pay for his sister's trip to Europe. I think that's very admirable, don't you? I could hardly kick him out, could I, when he's saving money for such a good cause?"

Her mother was very silent. Then she sighed. "Just be...careful, Ariel."

"Careful?"

"Is this like it was with Grayson?"

"Grayson? Oh, heavens no. Impossible. I'm not going to drop everything and run off with Jake, for heaven's sake. With Grayson, I was young and clueless."

"Uh-huh," her mother said, asking for more explanation.

"I mean, Jake's impossible," she continued, worrying out loud. "He's undependable and lazy—well, not really lazy, but particular about what he does and when he does it—and he'd never settle down. He's got women all over the place... Plus, I'm completely wrapped up in my work...and he is not the kind of man I would want. Not at all... So...what was the question again?" She felt over-heated—and not just because of the oven.

"It's not my place to tell you what to do, Ariel," her mother said, "but just keep your priorities straight, honey. I know it's tempting. Your father had a problem that way. I had to keep him on track. Your father was a grasshopper. No savings. No plan. I loved the man, but we saw things differently."

"I know, Mom, and I'm not like that," Ariel said, though she knew the powerful urge to forget herself in play had come from her father. Not that her mother didn't know how to have fun, but work came first. Because it had to. Back then, anyway. Not so much anymore...

"I know, dear. You're like me. Just...use your head. Hearts can be tricky."

"I will, Mom. Sure."

But the minute she hung up, she locked her mother's warning up and threw away the key, focusing on loading up ice and sodas and napkins to take out to the beach. She hadn't played volleyball since high school.

As she played volleyball, and at the Mexican restaurant they all went to for dinner, and throughout the raucous slumber party, Ariel focused on Jake and how much more he was than he seemed. The looks they exchanged and the fleeting touches seemed to build the pressure between them like a drumbeat. The fabric wall between their rooms had never been more thin, but with Jake's sister out on the porch and one girl or another popping into the bathroom every hour or so, Ariel didn't dare push through it and find her way to Jake's arms.

9

EARLY SUNDAY AFTERNOON, Penny and her friends left with regret, barely an hour before the yacht reception, which started at three. The girls had exhausted Ariel—taught her new dances, talked her ear off, made remarks about her dazed expression when she looked at Jake—"You're, like, totally, um, spaced."

Exactly.

She wanted to talk to Jake, to do something about her new feelings, but the afternoon reception loomed too large.

"You look great," Jake said, his eyes flaring in appreciation at the pale-yellow strapless cocktail dress with a sheer over-layer she'd chosen to wear. Then he frowned. "Except I don't think you should be showing all that...skin. You want these guys to work with you, not hit on you."

"Relax," she said, laughing lightly. "Aren't you always telling me I should *attract* business?"

"Yeah, with your mind," he said grumpily. "They see you like that and they'll go brainless."

"All the better to get their business," she said, then she slugged his arm. "Relax, Caveman, I'll wear a shawl." She smiled at his primitive possessiveness, even though he didn't own her beyond a few killer kisses. Killer kisses she wanted more of. She just wasn't sure....

She had to talk to him about it, but for now she had to focus on making important business contacts.

Jake looked perfect for the occasion. In his linen slacks and expensive plum silk shirt, he could easily pass for one of the business guys with a sailing habit he was going to introduce her to. He helped her put on a cream-colored silk shawl and they set off for the marina. In the car, she began to subtly wring her hands.

Jake glanced at her. "You're nervous."

"A little," she said, sitting on her hands.

"Relax. I'll introduce you around, mention you're a consultant, point out what you're doing with Water Gear. Then you just charm them like you did Brice."

"I know it'll be fine. I just...jitter." Her confidence about soliciting clients was still a bit shaky.

"I'll lob some softball questions," Jake said. He sounded casual, but purposeful, as if he was her partner in a business venture, not a guy heading out to kick back at a party.

"Thanks, Jake," she said, feeling better. "Don't worry about me. You should enjoy your evening."

"This is business for me, too. I expect to net some charters and maybe a few dive lessons with this crowd." He reached into his pocket and handed her a folded paper.

She opened it and found it was the calendar she'd created for him, substantially filled out. "You're using my chart."

"I laid it all out so I don't have to keep it in my head. And there are gaps in the next few months I want to fill today."

"That's the general idea. They call it plan-ning."

"Whatever. If it keeps me from double-booking something and getting yelled at, it's okay by me."

"You're welcome," she said.

He chuckled. "Okay, thanks." He gave her a level, serious look. This was the real Jake under the casual persona. Steady and thorough and never missing a thing. "I appreciate your setting this up for me. It helps."

"Being organized is good," she said, pushing the issue.

"Organized, but not anal. I barely set down that bike repair manual and it disappeared."

"It was in the middle of the floor."

"That's where it belonged. With the bike I was working on."

"Now that you mention it, working on bikes in the middle of the living room is a bad idea. Grease and sand and..."

"I didn't get a drop of grease on that floor.... Okay, I give. I'll move out to the sunporch when you're working."

"Wouldn't it be more convenient if you had a shop where you worked on bikes? Maybe a regular job doing it?"

"Working on bikes is just for fun."

"But isn't it tiring doing odd jobs all the time?"

"Sometimes."

Jake *did* want more. She knew it. This was definite progress. She just had to make him feel safe enough to go for it. "You know, when Brice opens up a second store, he'll need a manager.... Someone he trusts..."

"Are you crazy?" He shot her a look. "I could never

work for Brice. Teaching classes for him is tough enough."

"Just a thought."

"Look, I was joking when I said you could trade business advice for my cooking. I like my life."

"I just thought maybe you'd want something more...stable."

"If I do, I'll get it." He shot her a look. "Save the pep talk for your clients." He was smiling, but a muscle ticked in his jaw. "You're starting to sound like the Admiral."

"Sorry," she said. But he *was* thinking about more and that was good. Hope rose in her.

They pulled into the marina, got out and walked toward the yacht, which was festive with strings of Japanese lanterns and crowded with men and women talking, drinking and eating hors d'oeuvres from trays passed by waiters.

"Well, here I go," she said to Jake, as they headed on board.

"You'll knock 'em dead," he said in her ear, guiding her forward with a comforting hand at the small of her back.

Before long she seemed to be doing just that. Jake knew lots of people and smoothly eased her into each group, weaving her expertise into every conversation, so that it became natural to share amusing stories of her past successes and hand over business cards like Halloween candy.

It was as if Jake were her agent, gently promoting her, working the crowd at a Hollywood party. Remarkable. It was clear that people respected his expertise about

sailing and diving. She was surprised to learn he had a
degree in recreation education. She saw him filling in his
calendar some, and she managed to help him, too—in-
troducing him to a couple looking for a sailboat captain.

She had a hard time thinking of this smooth guy who
conversed comfortably with millionaires as the goofball
chasing a dog on the beach, throwing sand between his
legs for a sand castle, but she was so glad she'd discov-
ered him. She had lots in common with this side of Jake.

Still, despite Jake's help and all the cards she'd passed
out, the afternoon was fading and no lead had really
clicked for Ariel. Frustration mounted. She caught sight
of the manager of several trendy diners she wanted to
introduce herself to, so she followed him below decks at
a discreet distance. He went into the bathroom, so she
pretended to look at the sailing photos on one side of the
teak-accented cabin, waiting for him to emerge.

"Ariel?"

She turned to find Jake holding out a frosted glass. She
was pleased to see him. "No alcohol," she said, shaking
her head. "I have to keep my wits about me."

"The party's almost over. Come on. The sun is setting."

"There's a guy in the bathroom I want to snag."

"You're attracting business, remember, not stalking
it?"

"I guess a break won't hurt." Jake linked arms with
her and she felt that swoosh of lust and pleasure, a guilty
indulgence when she was supposed to be working. To
make up for it, she scanned the crowd for people she
needed to meet and was pleased to see she'd done all
she could do. The groups were sparse now.

Except for a guy in an extremely loud silk shirt, Ariel and Jake had the bow to themselves. "Look." Jake turned Ariel toward the ocean, where the setting sun glowed pink and orange on the horizon, its light turning the water silver, as if on some magical forge. The breeze lifted her hair like a gentle hand. The soft light gave everything a violet sheen. White things glowed—Jake's teeth and his eyes around the smoky-blue pupils, deepened to gray by the dusk. Ariel sucked in a breath. "It's so lovely."

"Absolutely," Jake said, but he was looking at her. He took her hand. "You're so pretty when you let go," he said.

"I shouldn't be letting go. I'm on duty here."

He pushed her hair away from her face. "My dad would love you. Never stop working, never let things slide."

"Your dad wasn't all wrong. Hard work has its rewards."

"Like what? Ulcers?"

"Like the satisfaction of a job well done. Like accomplishing things, making things happen. I love my work. I help people make their dreams come true."

"You're sure making Brice happy, and he's one cranky dude."

"What he wants is very possible. He's just been afraid to try. He needed proof. So I've done the market research, shown him the numbers and made a plan that's perfect for him. That's my strength—customizing my work to suit each client. We'll handle it step by step, so it doesn't scare Brice. This is a perfect time for him to expand...."

She glanced to the side and realized the man in the bright shirt was eavesdropping, a smile on his face. He was tall and big-bellied with white, longish hair and a ruddy complexion. In his Hawaiian shirt, he looked like Santa Claus on vacation.

Catching her looking, the man spoke. "Sounds like you love your job. Hard not to listen in on that much enthusiasm."

"I enjoy it, yes," she said. "Very much."

"Myron Becker." He shook her hand, then Jake's, as they introduced themselves. His grin was casual, but there was an alert intelligence in his eyes. "Don't let me interrupt you."

"That's all right," she said. "I was just talking business."

"You mentioned market research," Myron said. "One of my partners keeps at me about niche marketing. Know anything about that?"

Ariel explained what she knew and went on to discuss brand development and value streaming, while Myron nodded and Jake asked good questions. She was aware of him beside her, her partner, and she loved feeling like a couple.

"Very interesting, Miss Adams," Myron said.

"I'm sorry I've gone on and on," she said. "I get carried away."

"No, no. I've enjoyed it very much." Myron reached into his pocket for a card, which he handed her. "I like your attitude. I might want to hire you. Come see me tomorrow afternoon. Three o'clock. We'll talk." He patted her shoulder and left them.

Omigod. Ariel held her cool watching Becker depart,

but she said through her teeth. "I did it. I just scored a client."

"I know. You were stunning."

"I wasn't even trying to sell myself. I was just... talking. Oh, my. I have to jump up and down. *Right now.*"

"Hang on. Wait'll he's out of sight."

Ariel contented herself with looking down at Myron's card, hoping it didn't say *April Fool!* What she saw stunned her. "Oh. My. God. Myron Becker is the CEO of AutoWerks."

"That bowl full of jelly is the king of auto parts?"

"And he wants to hire me," she said softly.

"Looks like you scored."

"Big. I scored big. Really, really big."

"You sound surprised."

"The chances of me getting such a big account are a...a..."

"A slam dunk. He just had to meet you, that's all." Jake seemed so sure of her.... Abruptly, she noticed something different in his face—something she'd never seen before. It was closeness, intimacy. Gone was the barrier she'd seen when Jake had looked at Heather that first day. Jake was looking at her full in the face, offering up his feelings, his belief in her. His heart?

Ariel's resistance to being with Jake—really being with him—melted away. She felt sure...as if her mind and heart had moved from some painful, grinding gear, to a smooth, high-flying overdrive.

For the first time in forever, she didn't stop to think, make a pro-con list or second-guess herself. She just threw her arms around Jake and hugged him, practically bowling him over.

He laughed, caught his balance and gripped her around the waist. "Easy there," he said, setting her on her feet, looking puzzled, watchful. "What?"

"I want to..." *Kiss you, fall crazy in love with you.*

"What? You want to what?"

"This," she said and she kissed him, putting all of her heart in it.

"Oh, that," he murmured, breaking off for just a second. "That's not very professional," he said, glancing around the bow of the boat—empty now.

"I don't care. There's just the guy from Chick's Fun-Time Diners. I can call him later." She stood on tiptoes to mash her lips on Jake's.

This time he kissed back, making her tremble and nearly drop to the boat deck in weak-kneed surrender. They kissed for a long time, the only sound a gasp for air, a moan, a sigh. Finally, they separated, sucking in air, looking into each other's face with wonder.

"Are you sure?" Jake asked. "This is what you want?"

She nodded slowly, hoping she wasn't deluding herself. But look at Jake's face! This was no fling for him.

"Let's beat it out of here then, before I lose all control."

Ariel was almost willing to risk it. Her wild side was shouting and leaping for joy, completely out of control.

"I know a place I want to take you," Jake said.

Ariel nodded and they hurried to the stern of the boat to thank their host and leave. In a fever to be in Jake's arms, she was impatient when Jake stopped on the way home to buy a bottle of champagne, frustrated when he stopped at the house for a blanket, irritated when he searched for plastic cups—though she did take a second to yank off her panty hose.

At last, they walked the empty beach, arm-in-arm, toward Jake's place, Ariel so excited she was numb to the itch of sand on her instep. Her heart pounded so hard she was scared Jake could hear it over the wash of waves. She began to shake.

"You cold?" Jake said, pulling her more tightly to him.

"Not at all,". she said. "It's just nerves."

He gazed at her. "I know. I feel it, too. I don't think I've ever wanted a woman as much as I want you right now."

She saw they were headed toward a rocky outcropping. She had a painful thought. "I don't want to go where you've...you know..." *Been with another woman.*

"I come here to be alone," he said, leveling his gaze to hers. "And now with you." Exactly what she needed to hear.

Jake led her to a beautiful rock cave, sheltered from wind, the sand beige and smooth as powdered coffee creamer. The ocean spread out before them—nearby, but not close enough to reach them—shushing rhythmically, making the cave seem a cozy shelter from some storm.

Together they shook out the blanket, then sat face to face on it. She should have changed her clothes, she realized distantly. It wasn't like her to risk damaging something as delicate and expensive as this dress, but she hadn't wanted to waste a second at the house—barely thought of taking off her panty hose—and that just to have her toes free. This thoughtless behavior should trouble her, she knew, but then Jake popped the champagne cork and the sound echoed against the stone chamber like a shot—stopping all thoughts except those pertaining to here and now and the two of them together.

He poured the frothy liquid into two plastic glasses, letting it spill freely over the sides—a waste of what she recognized as expensive champagne, but it felt right. Everything was spilling out tonight—their feelings for each other, their hopes, and the possibility of so much more....

"To you," Jake said, clicking his glass against hers. "To your success and your happiness."

"To...you," she said, faltering because she wanted to say *to us*, but didn't quite feel ready.

They each took a solemn drink, staring into each other's eyes. The bubbles stung and flicked Ariel's face, like the little jolts of arousal zipping along her nerves. She felt a surge of panic—what was she doing?

Reading her mind, Jake tossed his champagne cup to the sand—hers, too—and pulled her into an embrace. Smart man. The kiss was slow and soft, coaxing her, opening her, obliterating her doubts with heat.

She welcomed the kiss and Jake's skilled tongue that slid into her, tasting, exploring. She used her tongue in his mouth, loving what she tasted and felt.

Her strapless dress took Jake barely a second to lower to her waist and he unhooked her bra, baring her breasts to the night.

She felt embarrassed to be nearly nude, but then Jake breathed the word, "Beautiful," and cupped both breasts, admiring them like a work of art or a gift, and it felt right to be naked in his hands.

She held her breath as he lowered his mouth to kiss the top of one breast, then the other, then to take one nipple between his lips, while gently squeezing the other between his thumb and a finger. The mixed sensation forced a half moan from her, harsh and primitive. Jolts of electric lust pulsed through her body and she had to feel Jake's arousal, to know he was as excited as she was.

Through his pants, she felt his rock-hard erection. He groaned, pushing against her palm. He had too many clothes on, she realized, and fumbled at his shirt buttons, wanting his chest warm against her own, his caged heart pounding against hers.

Jake stopped her hand, grabbed his silk shirt by the hem, yanked it over his head and tossed it carelessly to the sand before pulling her against him. His heart thudded and his lungs heaved just as hers were doing.

He lowered them gently to the blanket. Sand scraped Ariel's skin and she was aware of the blanket's wrinkles, the swells and lumps of pebbles and driftwood underneath, but all she cared about was the lovely weight of Jake's chest on hers, the delicious friction of his hair teasing her skin. They kissed for a long, long time.

Finally, Jake broke off the kiss. "I have to see you," he said and rolled them onto their sides so he could reach her zipper, open it and push the rest of her dress and panties off and away.

Modesty threatened at first, but no man had ever looked at Ariel with the desire she saw in Jake's eyes. She felt like a fairy-tale mermaid who had suddenly been given legs—uncertain and amazed, and oh, so grateful. Jake's hands slid down her hips, curved hungrily around her bottom. She was naked and open to the night and the sea air, feeling everything—the breeze, the sand, Jake's body, his fingertips, her own ticking desire.

Jake's erection pushed at her through his pants, which had to go. Now. She went for his belt. He helped her, then tossed off his pants.

Ariel gripped him hesitantly—he was smooth velvet over steel. She wasn't very good at stroking men like this, she knew, but Jake groaned and trembled, pushing upward through her curved fingers as if her touch was perfect. She heard Jake's words in her head. *Things work out.* For once, she'd believe that, she decided, and relaxed, moving her fingers the way she felt was good. ''Is this okay?'' she asked.

''Okay? If you don't stop, I'll go off right now and spoil everything.'' Then he surprised her by sliding a finger between her curls, giving her a jolt, as if she'd been touched by a frayed wire. She froze, riveted by the sensation.

''You're so wet,'' he murmured. ''And swollen. For me?''

She nodded, gasping for air, hyperventilating, no doubt, but she couldn't stop. She writhed against his fingers, afraid she might pass out.

''So, this is good?'' he asked, watching her reactions closely, the way he always watched her.

She nodded violently. Good. Yes, good. Good, good, good. She ached, throbbed, tingled with how good it was.

While his fingers explored her, Jake's mouth moved down her neck—kissing, licking, sucking—then reached her breast and its eager nipple, damp from his earlier caresses.

That was wonderful, but she was so far gone she wanted him inside her now, filling her, moving deep, really deep, inside all the way.

Then she remembered something dreadful. Protection. In her haze, she'd spaced it out. So not like her. Ariel thought these things out—had bedside condoms or a supply in her purse. "Do you have...what about...? Birth control," she gasped in despair.

Jake released her nipple, gently removed his finger, struggling for breath. He patted his pants, which lay beside her cheek, then reached inside. She heard a crinkling sound. Thank God. He must have grabbed condoms at the house.

But of course Jake would do that. This was a familiar situation for him. She wouldn't think about that, wouldn't even picture the women before her.

He'd never brought anyone here, though, she reminded herself. And he said he'd never wanted a woman so much. And there was closeness in his eyes. She could feel his heart thudding with as much power as her own. She clutched at him, desperate to hold on to this confidence that what they were sharing was special, unique.

"Hang on," Jake said, tearing at the package, which flipped from his fingers. "Damn."

Gratified that smooth Jake was so hot he was fumbling things, Ariel retrieved the wayward condom, tore into the package with her teeth and handed it to him.

He grinned. "Teamwork." He kept his eyes on her while he applied the condom. She felt so primal—gushng with wetness for him, reveling in this urge to mate, o unite with him. Then Jake parted her legs and pushed gently at her entrance.

She reached for his buttocks to force him in fast, but he held back, inching in, bit by delicious bit. She moaned and squirmed and tried to push him into her, but he maintained his slow approach, above her, arms extended, touching her only with his penis.

His slowness forced her to relax, to become aware of other things—the way the moonlight silvered the planes of his body, how the waves shushed and withdrew in an ancient rhythm that Jake seemed to match, how good he looked above her, stroking into her, as graceful as a dancer, pushing her closer and closer to a climax she knew would come like the waves surging beyond their bodies.

This would not be like the nervous times when her orgasm was elusive. She would reach the peak and go over, she knew, in Jake's arms, under his care. The throbbing need pulsed along her nerves, building and building to that coming leap of pleasure, like the waves of the moonlit ocean.

Feeling it approach, she reached up to pull him on top of her. She wanted his body tight against hers when she came.

Jake dropped to his elbows and his mouth met hers, hot and hungry. She lifted her hips, to give him more access to her, dug her fingers into the muscles of his behind, which were working madly for both their pleasure.

I'm yours. You're mine. She told him that with her body

and her heart. And she was sure she saw that message on his face, in his smoky, gleaming eyes.

He pushed hard once, twice, three more times, called her name in a groan, and pulsed inside her like the help less heartbeat of desire. Her own body let go, too, and she hurtled over the edge. They surged and bucked, slowing down gradually, until Jake released a heavy breath, tucked his arms around her and squeezed her tight. "My Ariel," he whispered in her ear.

Goose bumps raced down her body. *My Jake.* But she didn't have to say it out loud. They belonged to each other.

They breathed together for more long moments. She was about to remark on what had happened, but Jake sat up, pulling her with him. "Let's hit the waves," he said. Before she could object, he'd tugged her to her feet and they were running toward the dark water.

It wasn't even cold, and how could anything be more exquisite than moving her sexually relaxed muscles in the silky sea? The salt of their own juices joined with the salt of the sea in a primordial mix that felt carnal and right.

They held each other loosely, mermaid and man, effortlessly floating, legs tangled, waves surging under them. Ariel looked across the ocean. It seemed huge and alive, a giant beast with slowly rolling muscles. She thought about all those metaphors about eternity and tides and waves....

Before long, under the white moon, in the gleaming water, they joined their bodies again, their mutual cries floating in the air like a night bird's song.

How had she become a woman who would make love

on a public beach, in the ocean? But she stopped that thought. For once she wouldn't think, she would *feel*. And she felt everything—the sand and stones beneath her feet, the brush of seaweed along her thighs a greeting, not an annoyance, the slosh of water, the green smell of life and always, Jake's body, his arms holding her, his legs twining with hers, his penis finding her, finding its place in her.

At the right moment, Jake pulled out and released himself into the sea—as she knew he would—still touching her, until she rocketed over the edge, clinging to his wet shoulders, letting him hold her until she was still.

10

JAKE WAS AWAKENED by the light smack of female fingers across his face. He opened his eyes and realized Ariel had whapped him one in her sleep. *Thanks, I needed that.*

They'd ended up in Ariel's bed after making love most of the night. He'd been surprised when she threw herself at him on the yacht, but glad. Watching her practically quiver with joy about snaring the AutoWerks guy, he'd been pleased he'd helped her, made her happy. And he realized he wanted to keep making her happy.

And what better way to make her happy than in bed? Not to mention the mind-bending pleasure it had given him.

Except now, in the clear light of day, he had to wonder if maybe he'd been selfish. Maybe she hadn't been in her right mind last night. Maybe he should have put on the brakes.

He looked down at her. She lay naked beside him, her hair smelling lightly of the sea, her legs twined with his. It was as if he'd dragged one of those enchanted creatures from an Irish folk tale—woman by day, seal by night...silkies, right?—into bed with him. Any minute, she'd turn back into a woman who wore pink nightgowns to bed instead of this creature who slept nude in a sandy twist of sheets and sea smells, a peaceful smile on her face.

He'd called her *his Ariel*. And meant it. At the time. Making love to her had been different than with other women. Something about the way she gave herself over to him, feeling everything with such intensity. It seemed to mean so much to her.

It meant something to him, too, but *that* much? He wasn't sure. He could envision her daytime expectations grimly gathering over him like a storm cloud over a sunny morning. His chest tightened, making it hard to breathe, and he had to get out. Gently, he extracted his legs from hers. She smacked her lips sweetly in sleep and turned over.

He'd go get breakfast. Yeah. That would clear his head. As he headed out the door, he grabbed his board—just in case the waves were good. Ariel would be out for a while anyway. After all that lovemaking, she'd need to catch up on some sleep, and he needed to think. He left her a note, so she wouldn't freak.

IN HER DREAM, Ariel was rolling around in a cement mixer. She woke with a yelp and found herself twisted into a sheet gritty with sand. When she closed her teeth, they ground in dirt. She was in her own bed, she realized, where she and Jake had ended their lovemaking in an exhausted tangle at 3:00 a.m. Now she was clammy and scratchy with salt and sand. When she sat up, pebbles rained down her arms. Gross.

And Jake was gone. She listened hard. He wasn't in the house, either. Was that a bad sign? She dragged herself out of the bed, pulled the sheets around her body, and stumbled out to see what had happened to her lover.

For that matter, what had happened to her? She felt like one of those enchanted people who spend their nights as hawks or jaguars or deer and wake up unable to remember what animal acts they'd committed.

But she knew what she'd done, all right. She and Jake had made love over and over—on the beach, in the ocean, and then in her bed. And now here she was and he was gone. Had he fled from what had happened?

Then she saw the note on the kitchen table. "Bringing back breakfast. Jake." He'd gone for food. Her heart rose. She'd been ready to assume the worst, but he'd been looking out for her. On the other hand, he hadn't signed the note "love." And why go out for breakfast when he was so adept at making it?

He probably wanted something celebratory. She forced herself to stop worrying and headed for the shower. She was sore and foggy from all the sex, but she knew she had to get on the Net to collect preliminary information about AutoWerks before her meeting with Myron Becker this afternoon. But she couldn't help wanting to fall into bed again with Jake. She couldn't get over how good they were together—how much a part of her he'd seemed.

She took a quick shower, then forced herself to get to work. That way, when Jake got back, she wouldn't feel guilty about a lovemaking break.

An hour later, Jake still hadn't returned. He could have driven to San Diego and back with breakfast by now. He was avoiding her. Sick inside, Ariel rummaged in the refrigerator for a muffin, fighting the urge to dissolve into tears.

Adams women keep on keeping on, she told herself, munching on the tasteless pastry. Jake was telling her something—*don't count on me*. Okay, she wouldn't. She couldn't stand the pain, and she sure as hell wasn't going to yell about promises she'd read only in his eyes, tasted in his kisses, felt in his body.

She had to protect herself. By the time Jake returned, she'd explained it all away as an excess of sexual tension and her excitement about AutoWerks. But her heart seemed frozen, as if ice water had trickled into her chest.

HE WAS REALLY LATE, Jake realized with a jolt of alarm. He'd hit some great waves and needed the thinking time. But when he looked at his watch and saw he'd been two hours, he knew Ariel would be mad.

Great. She'd probably cry and carry on. Women like Ariel expected you to be on time. She'd probably want to talk about their *relationship* and their *feelings* and their *future together*. Things that gave him a headache.

But he hadn't promised her any of that, had he? he asked himself, standing in line at the deli. Dammit. How could she expect so much? He would just calmly explain that they cared for each other, but they couldn't pressure each other. All the same, he bought two extra flavors of cream cheese and some expensive lox to make up for being late.

As he drove home, he kicked himself for writing that note. He hated to be pinned down. But he'd known she'd panic when she found him gone. And now she'd hassle him for being late. All because he'd been thought-ful enough to leave word where he was.

Still fuming, he reached home, marched in, braced his board against the wall and plopped the deli bags on the table—two huge ones—he'd overdone it on the bagels. "Sorry I'm late," he said belligerently.

"You didn't specify when you'd be back," she said mildly, not even looking up from her computer.

"Aren't you going to yell at me?" he said, going to stand in front of her.

"Why should I? You brought breakfast like you said you would. End of story."

"Look, Ariel, I caught some waves and time slipped away. That's how it is with me."

She kept typing for a few seconds, but when she looked up her green eyes sparked with anger. He felt abruptly better, less guilty. "No matter what you may think, Jake, I have not been collecting lint and twigs."

"Lint and twigs?"

"Nesting, remember? Your big fear from a roommate you sleep with? Last night we had a simple little thing..." she hit the word *thing* hard. Thing? He'd say it was mind-bending. At the very least the earth had moved, but okay, if she wanted to minimize...

"And that's that," she continued. "Chalk it up to a crazy night of celebration and too much champagne."

"Too much champagne? We barely drank a swallow."

She shrugged. "The point is that you don't have to worry about things getting *complicated.* I know what's what. And that's that."

"Huh?"

"Forget it. You know what I mean."

Did he? It didn't matter. She'd handled this perfectly. No pressure. No expectations. That was good, right? He pushed away a twinge of irritation. "How about I warm you up a bagel? Blueberry or onion cream cheese?"

"Neither, thank you. I already ate."

"I said I'd bring breakfast."

"I've been up for two hours, Jake."

He didn't like the rigid set of her shoulders, the frostiness in her voice. He pulled up a chair beside her. "So, let me make it up to you. Isn't it about time to take a break? The pause that refreshes? Maybe build up an appetite?" He put his arm across her shoulder.

She shrugged it away. "I don't think that's a good idea." She turned to him, deadly serious. "We got it out of our system last night. Let's leave it at that." Was there a wobble in her voice? God, he hoped so. Otherwise, she was treating him like an overloud TV interrupting her work.

"You think? If you're sure.... Are you sure?"

"Absolutely."

"You mean for today or...?"

"For good. Neither of us wants this to get complicated."

"That's true. Okay then." He stood and looked down at her. She was typing away again like she'd just declined an offer to build a sand castle, not some terrific hours of great sex.

Wow. That was fast. It was probably best, if she was going to get all clingy and demanding—and that would definitely be her mode, for all her pretense at calm rationality. So, this was the best outcome. He should be relieved.

But he wasn't. He felt...let down...and disappointed. Maybe he was getting older, wanting things he could count on. Nah. He was as young as he'd ever been. As good on a board, as hot on a bike, as smooth on a sailboat as ever. He certainly wouldn't let a woman slow him down no matter how interesting she was.

Now what? He wandered into the kitchen for a bagel. God, there were enough for ten people in the bags. He'd take some over to Brice's. He needed to talk to the guy about the upcoming charters. Plus, Brice kept blowing off the community college professor who wanted to link up with Water Gear for a class on the physics of scuba. Jake wasn't looking forward to the disagreement, but he needed something to distract him from the urge to talk Ariel back into bed.

Maybe he'd get busy on that wall between their rooms. He sure as hell wouldn't plow through a wall for sex. Not even sex with Ariel.

Of course, he could always use the door.

ARIEL TOOLED HOME from the city that evening, so happy she felt as if she were floating above the ground in some kind of hovercraft. After the painful discussion with Jake, she'd buried herself in preparations for the meeting with Becker and it had gone perfectly.

Becker liked her energy and her dedication, which he said were the hallmarks of his own success, and had hired her, offering her a hefty retainer. On top of that, she'd rented office space in the very building she'd had her eye on.

It had seemed like fate when she'd pulled up to find a man hanging a "space available" sign from the building's window—even more so when she learned renters from a right-sized office space had disappeared, lease payments overdue, and the harried lease agent wanted to deal. She agreed to take over the payments, pay for the painting and small repairs herself and he'd offered her a screaming deal.

So she'd plunked down her first-month's AutoWerks retainer and now she had the office of her dreams. With a view and everything. She couldn't believe it. It was a little risky, but she had a good feeling about AutoWerks and she desperately needed to get out of the cramped beach house and somewhere closer to the corporate offices of her client. Her *giant* client.

Now she found herself racing home to tell Jake. Probably a sign that she was too attached to a man who didn't care enough about her to kiss her awake in the morning.

Still, in a way, she owed this success to Jake, who'd introduced her to Brice and arranged for her to meet Myron Becker. His advice about easing up had probably led to her ability to convince both clients to work with her.

Oh, who cares why? Right now she just wanted to see Jake's face when she told him her news. She hoped he'd be home. When she'd left, he'd been hammering up the Sheetrock between the two bedrooms—something she'd wanted him to do forever, but now it made her sad. It meant things were really over.

From the sunporch, she heard music and movement. He was home. Her heart rose. She found him at the kitchen table in swim trunks, squirting white frosting onto a chocolate layer cake, which had filled the cottage with its rich, warm aroma.

"Hey, Ariel," he said, glancing up at her. He'd adjusted to the change in their relationship with annoying ease, it seemed, which proved it was the right thing to do...probably.

"Smells good," she said, coming closer. She read what he was writing in white frosting: *Congrats, Ariel!* "But what if I hadn't gotten the job?"

"Of course you got it," he said simply.

"And you made me a cake." Her heart warmed.

"I'm still your roommate," he said. "You get the first piece." He picked up a knife and cut a wedge he placed on a paper plate.

She moved even closer to him, inhaled his coconut-and-man scent, along with the warm chocolate, took in the light bristle of his blond beard emerging, the slight dimple in his cheek.

"I couldn't wait to get home to tell you, Jake. I wanted to thank you for all you did."

"You did it yourself," he said. "I just opened a couple of doors."

"I got an amazing retainer and I put money down on an office and signed a lease. It's absolutely perfect."

"That's great. Here, taste," Jake said, holding out a forkful of cake. "You won't believe what makes this so moist."

But she didn't care about the cake. She only cared about the man who'd made it for her. The man she loved. She took in his eyes, fanned by sun wrinkles, flecked with indigo, and his mouth, built wide for grinning. He loved her, too. She could see it in his face. This morning, he'd just gotten scared. She'd been scared, too—so scared she'd backed out too fast.

She could tell Jake had picked up her mood because the fork he held wavered, then dipped, and the bite dropped to the floor. He took a step closer. She held still, starting to tremble.

"I've been thinking about this morning," she said.

"Don't," he said. "Don't think. That's what got me in trouble." He let the fork hit the floor, too, and yanked her into his arms. "I can't let you go," he said into her hair.

"Me neither," she said, so happy to be in his arms.

Jake's heart thumped against her chest. And then his mouth was on her, hard and hungry. Desire poured through her like thick syrup. She held tight to his bare back, wishing her clothes were gone so she could feel his chest against her breasts. She kicked off her shoes, heard them hit the wall.

"I want in you," he said, walking her backward through the living room, heading, she knew, for the bed. His fingers worked the buttons on her suit jacket.

"Yes," she said. "Inside me." *All the way.*

She banged something metal with her heel and felt wetness—she'd hit a paint tray, no doubt—but she didn't care. She kept moving, shutting out sensible thought.

They fell together on the bed, both tearing at her clothes. Her zipper snagged, got jerked open, the seam of her skirt tore. Jake tugged her panty hose away—ruining them, of course, but they were cheap. She noticed fleetingly that her foot was covered in Navajo white, which had smeared onto Jake's calves. Somewhere in there, Jake lost his trunks, and they were naked, and it was like coming home.

Jake couldn't believe he had Ariel in his arms again. He felt as though he'd been starving for her—her flowery scent, her tight body, her smooth skin, the round swell of her breasts, her pink nipples and her sweet little mouth. She reached for him and he almost shot off at just her touch. He wanted in, though, wanted to bury himself in her, make her his.

He needed a condom. Now. "Hold it." He staggered to his feet and to the wall he'd started to tack together. Right now, that Sheetrock stood between him and what he needed, so he jerked it off the studs and tossed it away to Ariel's shocked gasp, then giddy laugh. He loved making her laugh.

He stepped over the baseboard, grabbed what he needed from his nightstand, then lunged back to Ariel's bed.

Except those few cooling seconds had got her thinking again. Uh-oh. He had to keep her in sync with him, deep into what they were doing. He kissed her mouth, her neck, then lower, kissing her skin as he headed down to where he could offer her that special pleasure—and really taste her.

"Oh," she said, gripping his hair, realizing what he intended. "I don't think I—" Before she could finish her worry, he found her with his tongue and softly dabbed.

She went rigid, gasped for air and then quivered into the feeling. She was into it. Good. He gripped her hips, so he could keep his mouth where it needed to be and he began to lick her there.

As he did so, he felt the oddest sensation—a sort of calm certainty that this was where he belonged. He enjoyed tasting women, knew they loved it, but with Ariel he felt the pleasure of it in his bones—each twinge, every lunge made his heart swell with the desire to give her more and more. He slid his tongue inside, then out.

"Oh, oh, oh." Her voice was weak with wanting.

He focused on that sound, wanting more of it, wanting that final gasp of desperate pleasure, knowing she was depending on him to get her there. For all their differences in daily life, in bed they were a matched team, knowing each other as if they inhabited each other's skin.

Ariel pushed up against him, calling his name with such yearning that warmth rushed through him. His own release seemed distant, willingly set aside in favor of her fulfillment. Again he had that sense of rightness...as if they were two halves of a whole. The words *soul mate* rose in his mind but that was just the magic of lovemaking, the natural consequences of this much intimacy. Probably.

Then Ariel signaled her climax with a drawn-out "Oh, Jake," like a cry of relief and gratitude and amazement. He stilled his tongue and felt her orgasm ripple through her body. He held her gently. Her fingers, which had been gripping his hair, loosened.

When she was still, he looked up at her and saw how beautiful she was, her pale skin lightly tanned around the edges of what her modest swimsuit covered. Her chest had a post-orgasmic flush, and her nipples were still tight. And she wore a smile—a sweet, relaxed, satisfied smile.

Even in the trembling aftermath of her orgasm, she was reaching for him and he knew, looking up at her, that he loved her. He loved her body, loved making love to her, loved how she thought, who she was, with all her focus and energy. He slid up her body and kissed her, his own need beginning to pulse through him.

She broke off the kiss and looked at him, her eyes wide. "How do you know exactly what to do? I didn't even know where I was half the time."

"You were right here," he said, squeezing her. "And so was I." He brushed her hair away from her face, perspiration making a strand cling to her forehead. "Now I want right here," he said and pushed himself at her entrance.

"Oh, please," she said, practically begging.

He quickly applied a condom and found his way where he belonged. Again he had the sensation of being part of her body—her warm, wet tightness, shaped just for him, muscled ridges hugging every inch, pulling him in, wanting him all the way there.

They worked together, pumping hard up that climb, striving, reaching, the rhythm taking over as the best wave ever surfed through them, tossing them together onto the sensual shore, both slick with sweat, their hearts pounding in perfect rhythm, hers a bit softer than his.

"I love you, Jake," Ariel said, the words like a prayer.

"Me, too," he said, squeezing his eyes tight. "I love you, too." He knew that was a promise—that he'd stay, that he'd be there for her, that they'd be together.

Panic swelled. What had he done? But Ariel was a sensible woman. Surely, she wouldn't get clingy and demanding. She'd said she wasn't nesting. She'd accepted him for who he was. Wasn't that what she'd promised him when she fell into his bed again?

He had the urge to escape, to move to his own bed and stretch out—just a few feet away through the wallboard he'd torn off the studs. Except Ariel had a death grip on his body—her arms around him, her legs twined so tightly he'd never get out, not even to go to the bathroom—and he realized that when he'd torn down that wallboard, he'd torn down all the walls between them.

11

THE FIRST THING Ariel noticed the next morning was that Jake was gone again. She panicked, pawing at the empty space. Was he off surfing, escaping from her again? Then she heard whistling and smelled garlic and realized he was cooking. Thank God.

She looked at the clock. Nine. She'd probably managed two hours of sleep total. She thought simultaneously of the AutoWerks project and of the man in the kitchen fixing her food. She wanted both, but her body felt too weary for sex and her mind too fuzzy for work.

She felt a flash of anxiety. Had she messed everything up? No. Their lovemaking had been more solid, more intense than the night before. This was more than a joining of bodies; it was a blending of spirits. Jake had felt it, too. She'd read it in his eyes, heard it in his voice, felt it in the way he held her, the way his tongue found her and stayed like it belonged.

He'd held her tight all night, too, tucked himself around her as if he was afraid to let her go. She looked at the open wall and smiled. Jake had ripped it down himself. What could be a clearer message than that?

He was changing. Settling down. He'd just needed someone stable to help him realize it. She pulled herself to the edge of the bed, tried to clear her head, then found her robe and padded out to the kitchen.

"Omelets with smoked salmon," he said, carrying two steaming plates to the table.

She sat at her place.

"Fish is brain food. I figured you'd need it for your work." He set her plate before her with a gentle plunk.

"Thanks, Jake." She gripped his wrist, looked up at him, "Last night was..."

"Yeah, it was," he said. He was smiling, but she caught the flicker of anxiety, which stood out on Jake's face like volcanic rock on a white-sand beach.

"We just have to give ourselves time to get used to this."

"Sure," he said. "Time." As if to silence any doubts he bent down to kiss her. There it was, that rush of desire that made her so sure they were right together. It will be okay, she told herself. Like Jake said, things work out.

They enjoyed a leisurely breakfast, glancing up at each other and smiling. A little tentative, she thought, but they had to get used to it.

After breakfast, Ariel got busy and Jake made himself scarce, working on the bathroom floor with uncharacteristic focus, declining a beach visit with Rickie and Lucky, and keeping the stereo low. Two women left messages that he didn't pick up. What would he do about all his women?

Despite how much work she had to do, Ariel kept getting lost in thought about Jake. Would he move in for good? Should he? They should talk about it, but she dreaded the conversation. Everything seemed so tentative.

She watched the fish swim and swirl across her computer screen—after the scuba experience, she'd changed the screensaver from a rolling banner of *keep on keeping on* to the underwater setting. Her computer dropped into screensaver again and again.

She thought about her checklist for her future husband—the man so clear in her mind she would recognize his voice when she heard it. Jake had a great voice. And he did care about her needs, like her dream man. Look how he'd treated her in bed, and he cooked for her constantly. She'd never dreamed of Mr. Wonderful being able to cook.

But what about a career? And ambition? Jake was a big zero there. *When I need it, I'll get it,* he'd said about getting a job. Maybe now he needed it. He said he didn't want to work for Brice, but what if he had his own shop? Not as a competitor to Brice, of course, but something to do with water sports.

She found the newspaper and looked through the classified ads. Before long she'd circled four listings—a sailing store, a surf shop and two charter boat businesses. She'd check them out. All Jake needed was a little boost and he'd learn the joys of settling into something, building on work he loved. That was a way she could help him.

FIVE DAYS LATER, Ariel headed home from an amazing day in the city. She'd accomplished a lot. First, there'd been a three-hour meeting with AutoWerks' L.A. management team explaining the proposal she'd somehow managed to cobble together despite a lack of sleep—Jake seemed to consider it a personal challenge to keep her in bed. The team liked her work and Becker had beamed her his Santa-Claus smile. He needed a little more marketing information that she would put together tonight and deliver tomorrow. He would take her report to a planning meeting with the New York office later in the week.

She'd promised to be available for questions and given him another card. Soon she'd be printing up new ones with her new office address and phone, as well as the number for the cell phone she felt rich enough to activate again.

To further stoke her enthusiasm, she'd cruised by her new office and gotten the weary leasing agent to show her the space again. She envisioned how it would look. *A seascape here. Brass coat hanger there. Floor-to-ceiling bookshelves on this wall. Maybe a small fountain in that corner.... No, no. A fish tank—saltwater. Yeah.*

After that, she'd checked out the business possibilities she'd found for Jake. The charter boat companies had sounded flaky on the phone, and the surf shop was too commercial for him. The sailing store would be too much, she saw right away, but the owner had a brother with a scuba shop who wanted to ease into retirement. The guy would probably let Jake buy in and take over gradually. She'd arranged a meeting between the guy and Jake for tomorrow afternoon and she couldn't wait to tell him.

Jake was applying primer to the front of the beach house when she returned. He was off the ladder in an instant, pulling her into his arms.

She didn't even care about the paint that might get on her suit. "I have great news," she told him.

"You can tell me in bed. I listen so much better when you're naked." He pulled her by the hand.

"But I have work to do," she said, stumbling over the threshold, laughter bubbling to her lips. *Work, schmerk.* She'd never felt this utterly wanted before.

"All work and no play makes Ariel a nervous wreck," Jake said, turning to unbutton her jacket.

"All play and no work makes Ariel lose clients," she said, tugging his T-shirt over his head.

"But more play and less work got you clients," he said, starting on her blouse buttons. "I lined up a special dive tomorrow. A friend's taking a boat out to the Point Loma kelp beds—as great as the offshore islands. The most incredible forest of towering kelp, terrific reefs. You won't believe it."

"I can't, Jake. I have some follow-up for AutoWerks."

"Can't you do it later?"

"It's for tomorrow. Plus, I—"

His kiss stopped her words and her mind went blank, except for what his fingers were doing to her through her underwear. *Oh. My. Goodness.*

The scuba shop floated into her awareness and she managed to break off the kiss long enough to say, "I have news for you, too."

"You're about to come. That's not news," he said, sliding his fingers to the spot that drove her mad.

"No, no." She pulled away and told him about the scuba shop and the meeting she'd scheduled for him at four.

"I'm not interested in owning a business, Ariel." He sounded exasperated, but only momentarily. He reached for her again, snapped her bra off in quick moves, then cupped her breasts.

"But you'll like this guy," she gasped out. His hands

felt so good on her skin. "He reminds me of Brice and he has a great idea for a scuba club—a connection with a...a...a..." He was doing something amazing with his tongue on her nipple. "...tourist agency so you could arrange trips to Mexico to d-d-ive."

"You're relentless, you know?" he said, lifting his face from her breasts. "If I weren't so hot, I'd be pissed."

"Relentlessness is one of my most endearing traits," she said, feeling faint.

"In bed maybe..." He paused, caught by her expression. Behind the lust was her hope for him and he must have seen that. "Okay. We can make it back from the dive before four, I guess."

"Terrific," she said and put her arms around him.

"Of course I'd say anything to get into your pants right now," he said, shoving her skirt and everything underneath to the floor.

"Mmm," she said, pushing down his trunks. "But I still have to finish my report. I don't see how we can dive, too."

"Do it later tonight. You won't believe how gorgeous this spot is. It's like an undersea hanging garden, with an incredible menagerie. Electric rays, huge fish, groupers as big as my Beetle."

"Really?"

"Really," he said, his hand sliding down her back to hold her bottom tightly against him, rubbing himself against her softest spot. Good sense began to fade.

"I can probably do the work in two hours," she said, "but we have to drop it at AutoWerks before we go."

"E-mail it tonight." He lifted her up and pushed into her with one quick thrust.

Oh. My. Goodness. E-mail, Morse Code, smoke signals. She didn't care how she got it to him. Right now nothing mattered except the exquisite pleasure of Jake inside her, pushing deeper, striving for completion. Somehow they made their way to the bedroom and Jake found a condom just in time.

BLEARY-EYED, Ariel checked her messages at a pay phone at the San Diego dock before they headed off to the dive. She must be losing her mind. She'd dragged herself from a sleeping Jake at 2:00 a.m. to put the finishing touches on her report and e-mail it to Myron. She'd had a terrible time concentrating. And it wasn't even Jake's fault. She couldn't stop thinking about his hands and mouth and what they'd done to her. She'd become obsessed.

I have to get some balance, she thought, hanging up the phone with a sigh. Her head felt plugged with cotton. Jake beamed at her—he was delighted that he'd altered her ways—but his face was filled with so much love that she couldn't even be irritated at his assumption that this was good for her.

They boarded the dive boat and roared toward Point Loma. Ariel went below to use the head and when she climbed back on deck, she heard Jake talking with Dave, the owner of the boat. Dave said something about Miami, and Jake answered, "Yeah, I was thinking of moving out to there. Warm water would be great. A lot of charters run out of the Bahamas."

"There's plenty to do," Dave said. "My cousin works whenever he wants to."

Jake nodded. He was considering the idea, she could

tell, and her heart lurched. He wanted to move to Florida?

"What's up?" she asked, moving close to him.

"Nothing, just shooting the breeze."

Dave went to the back of the boat to arrange the gear. As soon as he was out of earshot, she said, "You're moving to Florida?"

"It's just talk." He hugged her. "We're together now. I'm not going anywhere."

Just yet. She could hear it in his voice, see it in his face and felt queasy.

They got busy preparing to dive and the excitement of it distracted her from her worries about Jake and AutoWerks and her imbalanced life. And once she was underwater, it was easy to focus on the wonder of what she was seeing. She loved holding Jake's hand and looking upward through the giant, gently swaying kelp trees, the high coral hills, to the light shimmering above them. It was like being in some fairy-tale forest, almost a holy place. A giant fish swam lazily among the kelp, taking all this beauty for granted. She looked at Jake, who was looking at her. What an amazing thing to share.

When they reached the surface, the crew had news— some gray whales had surfaced not far away.

"You'll love this," Jake said. "You won't believe how big and beautiful they are."

"But we need to get back," she said, checking the time on his diver's watch.

"We'll make it, don't worry," he said.

It hardly mattered, since Dave had turned the boat away from shore and roared off. She worried as they skimmed the water, but Jake kept squeezing her hand. *It'll be all right.*

The whales were awe-inspiring. Diving, surfacing, spouting and rolling with majestic grace, as if putting on a show for them. She spotted a baby swimming close to its mother. "Look!" she pointed for Jake's benefit.

Jake looked and smiled. "Cool."

"Cool? It's amazing," Ariel said and Jake realized he could look into Ariel's wide, eager eyes for a long, long time. She was interested in everything, too, once you got her attention. He couldn't wait to teach her to surf.

She was loosening up day by day. It would take just a little time and she'd forget about trying to push him into things like this stupid business idea she had. If he felt aimless, which he did from time to time, he'd volunteer somewhere—become a Big Brother or something.

Ariel would stop hassling him, once she really eased up. And he had to admit a little organization made him feel better. He didn't spend nearly so much time hunting down his keys or missing classes as he used to. Clean dishes and utensils in predictable places made cooking a hell of a lot more fun, too.

When she put her small hand in his he felt the power of her trust and he never wanted to let her down. Ever.

What was she saying now? Something more about the calf's expression.... He looked into her flashing eyes and laughing mouth and the lust for her rose in him again.

"They're quite intelligent, you know," Ariel said, then caught herself. She'd been babbling on and on, describing something Jake had been standing right beside her watching. "I'm sorry to carry on so much."

"I like it when you get excited...in every way," he said

and he kissed her, soft and slow. "You taste salty. If these guys weren't on deck I'd strip you down and lick every inch of salt off you."

She shivered with the thrill of it. She could feel Jake's erection against her stomach through the Neoprene. She couldn't wait to get home and get them both out of these suits and—

Hold it! Jake had an appointment at the scuba shop at four o'clock. "What time is it?" She grabbed Jake's wrist and read the time. "It's already two. We won't make it to the shop by four."

"Another day." He shrugged.

"I scheduled the meeting. We have to call. Dave, do you have a cell phone we can borrow?"

"Battery's gone," Dave said. "Is there a problem?"

"No," Jake said.

"Yes," Ariel argued.

"Relax. We'll call him when we get to the marina."

"Can't we use your radio?" Ariel asked Dave.

"Forget it," Jake said, waving Dave off. "That's for emergencies," he told her, frowning. "Just relax."

"I can't relax. We have an appointment."

"So we'll make another one. Would you trade seeing that baby whale with its mother for a business meeting?"

"We could have had both."

He made an impatient noise, shrugged, and looked out to sea. Why did he blow off anything he didn't feel like doing? So childish. And now he was acting hurt. It was all well and good to enjoy life, but you had to be responsible, too.

As soon as they hit the slip, Ariel bounded off the deck

and hurried down the pier to the pay phone. It was already four-thirty. The shop owner, who'd given up a golf game to wait for Jake, was miffed, but polite. "Let me put Jake on the phone and you can set another meeting."

To her irritation, Jake took the guy's number and told him he'd call later, then ended the call.

"What do you mean you'll call him later? Go out there tomorrow, for heaven's sake."

"If this is supposed to work out, it will."

"But..." She looked into his face. It wore that *no trespassing* expression she'd seen when he'd looked at Heather way back when. "You don't even want to meet the guy, do you?"

"I told you I would," he said.

"But you don't want to."

"I like my life the way it is, Ariel."

"Then why did you say you'd go? Don't answer that." *I'd do anything to get in your pants.* She'd thought it was a joke.

"Look, Ariel..." he said.

"Forget it. I've got to check messages." She turned to the phone, wanting to hide her disappointment.

"Wait until we get home, would you?"

"No," she snapped. "I've waited long enough." She'd had enough of Jake twisting her arm to act against her instincts. There were four messages. Her heart began to pound as Myron Becker's voice came on. *Uh, Ariel, had a couple questions on your marketing numbers. Looks like a page or two is missing. I'll be at this number for another hour. Call me.*

He'd called at 8:00 a.m. Oh, God. The next message

was at nine-thirty. *Still waiting on the missing pages. And I wanted to ask you about the short-term priorities piece. We're thinking of a slight shift and don't know how that will play out. Call me. By noon. Use my cell.* He left the number.

Ariel began to feel sick. The third message, at twelve-thirty, was tinged with anger and ended with the fact he was leaving at five-thirty for New York and he expected to hear from her before then.

The last call came from the airport. *This is unacceptable. I need you to be available. My managers weren't keen on hiring a consultant in the first place. I'll pay you for your preliminary plan, but I don't think this will work out.*

Ariel hung up the phone without deleting the message.

"What's wrong?" Jake said.

"Becker's been trying to reach me all day. Two pages of the report were missing and he had questions. I wasn't there. Now he doesn't want to work with me."

"Come on. He fired you over a few-hour delay?"

"I told him I'd be available. Absolutely. I told him *absolutely.* And I just disappeared. Even if I'd gotten back to him, I would have needed my computer to answer his questions. I completely screwed up."

She felt sick and dizzy and angry—at Jake for being so cavalier about her work and at herself for letting him sway her. "I should never have gone. I knew it. It was irresponsible."

"Come on. You're allowed to have some fun."

"*Some* fun, yeah. But not 24/7, like you seem to do. How could I have been so stupid?"

"Why would you want to work for a guy who'd cut you off over one misunderstanding?"

"For every reason in the world. Because he's an important man. Because I was counting on his retainer. Because I need his referrals. This is a new relationship. Everything counts when it's new. He wasn't sure about me. I was proving myself."

"So call the guy back. Tell him it was my fault. Or let me tell him."

"You've done enough," she snapped, then spoke more calmly. "I'll handle it. It's my mistake. I'll call ahead to New York and leave a message."

If Becker didn't take her back, she'd have to give up her office. Lose the deposit. She'd known better than to jump on that office so soon. *Don't spend what you don't have. There's no such thing as a sure thing.* She knew all those truths—had learned them from her mother and lived by them—but she'd fallen in love with Jake Renner and started acting on impulse without even realizing it. *Keep your priorities straight,* her mother had warned her. She'd been so right. Ariel had let herself lose focus. *Is this like with Grayson?* her mother had asked. Yes, it was, she saw now. She'd figuratively run away with Jake, just as she'd nearly literally done with Grayson.

"It'll work out," Jake said.

"Don't give me that," she said, her anger flaring, her good sense snapping back into place with a hard click. "Things work out when I work at them, not when I let them just happen. I don't float through life like you, Jake. I work for success."

His eyes went cold. "So let's get you back to it then."

They didn't speak on the drive home. Ariel kept wanting to say something to fix it, but she couldn't figure how. It was completely wrong.

She looked at Jake. A muscle ticked in his jaw. He didn't understand her. She'd been kidding herself thinking they could work things out, that love would find a way.

She should have stuck with her checklist—her whole checklist. She knew what kind of man she needed—a kind, hard-working, responsible, loving partner who wanted the same things she did, who would strive for them with her—not an arrogant, stubborn, overgrown adolescent who elevated play into some kind of religion as an excuse to be irresponsible.

When they got to the house, Ariel left a message for Myron on his New York voicemail.

Then she e-mailed him the missing pages of the report and tried to script out what she'd say about her unacceptable and uncharacteristic behavior when she finally got him on the phone.

She blocked out her awareness that Jake was moving around her, chewed madly on her lip and focused on what she had to do. How had she forgotten what was important? How had she let this thing with Jake wash away her good sense, her focus, her goals? Her mother had been so right to warn her. She'd let her impulsive side—*thank you, Dad*—take over and disaster had struck.

She was startled when Jake appeared at her side and set before her a complex salad topped with avocado, sunflower seeds, mandarin oranges, crumbled bacon and blue cheese.

"Thank you," she said, looking up at him.

"Figured you needed food," he said.

"I'm sorry I got so angry," she said. "I was just shocked and this account means so much to me."

"You can fix it. If that's what you really want."

"Everything depends on this—my business, my future. Hell, even my office—that's out the window if I lose AutoWerks. I loved that building. It was perfect. Now I might lose it."

"You don't need another office. The sunporch will be great. If we extended the foundation, you'd have more space."

"The sunporch has no windows, Jake," she snapped, "in case you haven't noticed. You ripped out the screens and there's no Plexiglas in sight. I need a real office, not a sand trap."

"You'd rather fight city smog and traffic than work on the beach?"

"Cities are where business is supposed to be, Jake."

"That's your whole problem. You throw away what you have for how things are supposed to be. Look what's right outside your window." He rolled her task chair away from her desk in the corner and into the middle of the living room so she was looking out the front window. "You don't even let yourself enjoy the scenery while you work."

"I have to concentrate. The beach is...distracting."

"Exactly. Pleasure and beauty are just distractions to you. Look out there—sun and sand and waves and people—all those wonderful things and you hide away in the corner, burying yourself in work."

"That's not fair. I enjoy things when the time is right."

"Everything can't be timed. Take us. You think we're bad timing, right? That I'm just another distraction. Something that keeps you from almighty work."

"You don't respect my work."

"I respect it, but I don't worship it. And you shouldn't either. If I hadn't made you relax a little, you wouldn't have the clients you have right now."

"I earned those clients and I'm proud of it. Run from responsibility if you want, but don't try to convince me you're right. And don't expect me to join you."

"You think because I don't want to own a scuba shop I'm irresponsible? Look, my life works just fine for me."

"And mine works for me. There's nothing wrong with working for your dreams."

"That's the point. I'm living my dream, Ariel. You're just working for yours."

"That's bull. You want more than just hanging out at the beach. I know you do. You want a home, a place for all your junk—for a guy who hangs loose, you sure drag around a lot of equipment."

"What are you getting it?"

"I'm not your father telling you to buckle down and sail right or whatever. I'm trying to help you do something more you might like if you weren't so pigheaded."

"Leave my father out of it. And at least I admit I'm pigheaded. This is who I am, Ariel. Take it or leave it."

She looked at him for a long, painful moment. How could she take it? The struggle would be endless, with him tugging her away from what mattered to her, refusing to budge an inch. How long could she look at the bicycles against the wall, the scuba gear everywhere? He'd been working on the house for weeks and still wasn't close to finishing. And he was thinking about moving to Florida, for God's sake. She'd been in a trance.

"I think we should talk about this when we're both more calm," she said.

"It's okay," he said quietly. "I get it. We're done. I'll move in with Brice."

"You don't have to leave," she said, panicking at the thought. "Not right away, I mean."

"No. I should have moved out when you asked me the first time. It would have been the responsible thing." He flung the word *responsible* at her like a Frisbee aimed at her gut.

12

THAT WAS THAT, Jake thought, stomping out of the house for a swim to cool off. He was moving out after all—and it was his idea this time. He should have known Ariel would be trouble the minute she ran head-on into him in her business suit that first day. She was work-crazed, uptight and demanding. He'd known that from the start. But she was also eager and so fun to amaze.

He'd never stuck around for a relationship before, never wanted to, and now he knew why. It was one big pain in the ass.

He'd get over it. Move on. That was one good thing about growing up in the Navy. You knew how to move on.

He swam for a steady hour, but still felt that tightness in his chest, that burning emptiness in his stomach. Maybe he was just hungry.

He headed to his favorite place for a smoothie and a falafel, pleased to see a couple of surfing buddies hanging there. He hadn't seen these guys in a while—he'd been spending entirely too much time trying to straighten out Ariel.

There was a new girl behind the counter. Kiki, according to her name badge. Very cute. And the opposite of Ariel—a tall, long-limbed blonde with a lazy smile. She gave him the look.

He tried to return it, but failed miserably. The idea of being with her just made him tired. Panic flickered through him. Was he getting old after all?

He couldn't ditch the memory of Ariel's tight little body tucked against him in sleep. He craved her, felt sick with longing for her, even missed her bustle and chatter. He was a fool.

Okay, this was a normal reaction after a breakup—for most guys, anyway. Of course, he wasn't most guys. He'd left lots of things he loved and never before felt this ache in his bones like something permanent was broken.

When the smoothie came—smelling deliciously of raspberry and banana, with that earthy wheat-germ density—he could barely get down a swallow. And the falafel turned his stomach. Hell, Ariel had even ruined his appetite.

He had to do something—talk Brice into letting him stay there maybe. He stomped into the cottage—Ariel didn't even look up from where she was banging away at her computer sniffling—and threw some things into a bag. As he crammed clothes into his duffel, he saw that he *had* accumulated a lot of stuff. She'd been right about that. Screw it. He could sell it or give it away. He didn't need the stuff or the place to store it, or Ariel, or anything. He could start over any time. Anywhere.

Brice looked up from his adding machine when Jake walked in. "You look like you lost your last friend," he said. "I know that's not true because I still like you, ya bum."

Jake shrugged. He felt like he'd been slammed to the sand by the mother of all waves—scraped raw, inside and out.

"Trouble at the beach house?" Brice said, nodding slowly.

"You could say that."

"You'll work it out...." He held Jake's gaze. "You'd better. You need that woman to settle you down."

"Look who's talking. You haven't settled down."

"Just an act, my friend. Tears of a clown. Sylvia was my one love, and I let her go because I thought I was too young to limit myself to one woman." He shook his head.

"You could find someone else if you wanted to."

"Not like Sylvia. She's my one and only. You might find it hard to believe, but I'm not that easy to be with."

"Right." Brice was a stubborn, finicky old coot.

"But I'm fine. I'm happy. I have my shop."

But a shop didn't hold you tight at night, as if for life itself. A shop didn't sigh over your cooking or make smart-ass remarks about your work habits or hang up your towels before you'd even finished using them.

Yeah, but Ariel wanted to change him. He could see that look on her face. *Not good enough. Be better.* The same look his father gave him. It made him want to bust out, blow off the whole thing. "Can I crash on your couch for a few days, Brice?"

"If you cook—and buy the food—stay as long as you want."

That was set. For now, anyway. He wasn't looking forward to it, though. Brice's couch was lumpy as hell and the man snored like a chainsaw. He'd find another place soon and move on. That was best.

He and Ariel were like oil and vinegar. They made a

nice dressing, but it would take a paint spinner to keep them blended.

He'd bounce back, he knew. Like picking himself up from a wipeout. Except something seemed to have shifted inside him, something deep.

Okay, so he'd need more time. Maybe he *was* getting older. Maybe he needed a place for his junk. Maybe wipeouts were taking more of a toll....

ARIEL SPENT the entire next day leaving unanswered messages for Myron Becker and holding back tears about Jake. She forced herself to be sensible. Her misery was proof how smart she was to end it now. She'd been fooling herself to think Jake could ever be a compatible life partner.

When Myron hadn't called by three-thirty, she knew she had to take drastic measures. She called his secretary, Sue, who by now knew her voice. "I know he's ducking me, Sue. Tell him I'm coming to New York. I'm going to camp outside his office until he meets with me. Tell him that, please. I'll hold."

Sue sighed an enormous sigh, but sent Ariel to Muzak. After two full songs, she was back. "Twenty minutes, no more," she said. "Be here by three tomorrow."

As soon as Ariel hung up, she ordered a small thank-you flower arrangement for Sue. Okay, she had a chance. And this time she would not blow it. She paid for her ticket online and went to get something to eat before packing.

The beach house felt so empty with Jake gone. Funny, when she'd first moved here, she'd have given anything for this rich quiet. Now, she couldn't think without Jake's music, his whistle, his bang and clang and thump.

She opened the refrigerator, knowing she should eat, though her appetite was completely shot. The shelves bulged with leftovers from Jake's cooking. The sight made huge tears swell in her eyes. Never again would he hold out a forkful of *huevos whateveros* for her to sample, or butter her a muffin or bake her a cake. She shut the door and leaned against the fridge, trying to get herself under control. Hell, she was crying over leftovers.

The phone rang. Grateful for the distraction, she lunged for it, practically falling on her face on the desk. "Business Advantage," she said on a gasp.

"Ariel? It's Trudy. How's it going?" Her voice sounded far away and falsely cheerful.

"Trudy? Hi. Fine. Everything's fine," she said, not wanting to reveal the embarrassing screw-up she was in the midst of rectifying. "More or less. How about with you? Enjoying your fabulous new life?" She braced for more of the tales of quaint Greek villages and watercolor paintings that had peppered the two conversations they'd had in the past month.

To her amazement, Trudy gave a shaky sigh. "Actually, things are kind of rocky right now."

"You're kidding."

Trudy gave a strangled laugh. Definitely not a tinkle or a trill. "No. This will sound insane, but Paul and I spend every glorious minute together seeing amazing things..." then she whispered, "and I'm bored out of my mind."

"You're bored?"

"I miss Business Advantage. I have no purpose here.

Sure, I love Paul, but I don't *do* anything. And it's starting to affect me. We were at a cocktail party with some of his executives and the operations manager mentioned a turnover problem and I practically barnacled myself to the man advising him. Paul had to drag me away. I embarrassed him, can you believe it?"

"I'm sorry, Trudy."

"He was right—and wrong. We had this terrible fight, where I accused him of treating me like a brainless trophy. Can you imagine?"

"No." But she could. Trudy could be fierce.

"I think I wanted him to be angry at me. I wanted an excuse to...to...come home," she finished on a shaky breath. "Could you use a partner again, Ariel? I'll buy into the business, of course, but I'm dying out here. I was wrong. Love is not enough."

"Trudy...wow..." Trudy could bring in business, for certain. There would be less pressure on Ariel. Between the two of them they could afford an office, with or without AutoWerks. "That would be great," she said. "If you're sure, I mean."

"I learned my lesson," she said sadly. "People are who they are and love can't change that."

Ariel was about to agree—that was the lesson she'd learned from Jake—until she heard Trudy's shaky sigh. There was so much defeat and grief in the sound that Ariel knew this was wrong.

"Trudy, listen. As much as I would love to have you here, I think you should give yourself more time. Talk to Paul. Look for some middle ground, where you enjoy each other, but you can still contribute professionally."

Trudy was silent.

"Are you there?"

"I'm thinking," she said slowly.

"You changed your life overnight. You have to expect some fallout. Talk to him. If you love each other you'll find a way."

What was she saying? With Trudy's help, they could go back to Plan A and everything would be hunky-dory.

But Plan A didn't seem right anymore. Not for Trudy and maybe not for her. Love was powerful. That was another thing falling in love with Jake had taught her. "Things work themselves out," she said. Now she was channeling Jake. She felt her shoulders lift into a Jake shrug.

"When did you get so wise?" Trudy said.

"It's a long story." She hated when Jake was right.

Trudy promised to call again in a week to talk about coming back, but Ariel could hear the relief in her voice. She felt certain Trudy and Paul would work something out. She and Jake wouldn't be so lucky.

She started packing. In the bathroom, she found the toothpaste tube squeezed in the middle and missing its cap and beach towels mildewing on the newly tiled floor. Oh, Jake.

She leaned against the sink and began to cry. No more trashed-out bathrooms, bike gears on the kitchen table, sand and seawater on the wooden floors. And it just broke her heart. To torture herself further, she picked up his razor and sniffed that delicious coconut smell.

She heard the door open and her heart slammed in her chest. Jake was back. Maybe he felt as miserable as she did. Maybe they could compromise somehow....

But Jake was whistling. Whistling! He'd bounced back

already. Of course he would. Falling in love was no big deal to him. He came down the hall and stood in the doorway, looking so handsome, staring at her like always, interested and curious.

She hid his razor behind her back. "You need to get in here?" she said. "It's okay. I'm finished."

"Take your time."

"I'm just packing for New York. I leave tonight."

"I told you he'd give you another chance."

"He's giving me twenty minutes," she said. "Less than half an hour to get his business back." She planned to create an addendum to the report that would impress him with her attention to detail. She'd do it on the plane and at the hotel before her appointment.

"You're the most determined woman I know. You'll do it."

"I wish I had your confidence."

"You should." His eyes flared. "I've been trying to show you that. If you wouldn't get so uptight about everything, you'd do fine.... But that's old news." He smiled—a ghost of his broad, full-faced grin. So he hadn't bounced back yet either. She felt better not being alone in her misery.

"Your support has meant a lot, Jake." Her voice shook. She ached to move into his arms and let him soothe her.

His face softened, his eyes went smoky. Maybe he wanted the same thing. He reached to touch her cheek. She closed her eyes. Maybe he would kiss her and it would all work out....

"You've got something here," he said, showing the finger that had touched her cheek. "Shaving cream?"

She opened her eyes. Hell, he'd caught her sniffing his razor. Embarrassment and disappointment rushed through her. "Here!" She slapped his razor, sharp side up, into his palm. "And try to find the cap to the toothpaste," she said, brushing by him.

What was her problem? Jake wondered. He was just being nice, cleaning her off—okay, any excuse to touch her face—and she'd snarled at him. Over the toothpaste cap? And what was she doing with his razor, anyway?

Women.

He used the bathroom, then found Ariel in her room packing. He stood in the doorway watching her tight butt wiggle from closet to drawer to suitcase. He remembered how they'd teased each other when she'd unpacked a month ago, clutching those sexy white undies.

He'd thought he'd helped her, but she wasn't a bit less jittery than when he'd met her. He wanted to keep trying—to pull her into his arms, calm her, make slow, sweet love to her until she fell into a relaxed sleep.

But that was over. She'd be gone. She wouldn't be around to yell at him to lower his music or to moan in ecstasy over his muffins, or to fill his life with such joy....

"You need a ride to the airport?" Anything for more time.

She jerked up, surprised by his voice, and clutched her panties to her chest, just like that first day. "Supershuttle."

"Then I'll pick you up. When do you return?"

She resumed packing. "Not sure. If it goes well, I'll stay and work a few days."

"Why are you so mad?" he said. "I'm trying to help you."

She blew out a breath. A world of reasons flew by on her face, but all she said was, "I'm not mad really. Just...sad."

"We gave it a shot." He shrugged, the gesture making his whole body ache.

"Exactly," she said and brushed viciously at her cheeks, where tears gleamed. God, he'd made her cry. What a jerk.

"I'll finish the house and move all my stuff out while you're gone," he said. That would make it easy on her.

"Whatever." He'd never heard her sound bitter before and he didn't like it.

The place was so quiet after she left, he couldn't stand it. He decided to invite Penny out for the weekend. He'd tell her about the trip to Europe, since he'd just about earned the money. That should boost him out of this stubborn funk over Ariel. If that didn't work, he could just move to Florida.

ON FRIDAY NIGHT, Jake brought a virgin strawberry daiquiri to his sister, who sat on the sunporch, her feet up on the table, grinning out at the sunset.

He handed her the drink and she gulped a big mouthful. "Not too fast or you'll get brain freeze," he said.

"Gawd, Jake. You just can't stop telling me what to do."

"You always whined about it when we went to Dairy Queen." He sat beside her, sipping the triple-rum daiquiri he'd made to numb himself with.

"When I was eight," she said, taking another big gulp. "So, what's the good news you have for me?" She lowered her feet and faced him. "And why do you look so sad about it?"

"Sad? I'm not sad."

"The hell you're not."

"Don't swear." He held up his hand to block her objection. "I know you're almost seventeen and a woman and you can make choices about your language."

"What happened, Jake? And don't say 'nothing.' You don't have cancer, do you?"

"God, no. I had something...fall through...on me."

"It's Ariel, isn't it? She dumped you?"

"Dumped me? No...how did you...? Forget it." He shook his head. Penny thought she knew more than she had any right to know. "It was mutual. Now just let it go." He ended more forcefully than he'd meant.

"Okay, okay," she said. "But you'd better let her win the fight. You're getting old. Killer looks don't last forever."

"Drop it, please, or I'll start interviewing your dates."

"I give," she said.

Jake fumbled in his pocket for the much-folded "study abroad" brochure and thrust it at her. "Here."

"What's this?" She unfolded it.

"A present. From me to you. And don't worry about the cost. I set the money aside. I'm telling you now so you can plan on it before you start applying to colleges."

"You're paying for this? But, Jake, this is too much...I don't know what to say...."

"Say you're excited. And don't worry about the parents, Squirt. I'll make sure they know this will be good for you. There are chaperones and guided tours. It's completely safe."

"It's not the parents," she said. She looked up at him, troubled. "I can't let you spend this money on me."

"That's what money is for—to spend on people you love."

"I appreciate that, but..."

"But what? I know you want to go. You talked about it."

"But my friends are all going to UC Santa Barbara."

"Okay. So, you can go there when you get back."

"Yeah, but I..." She frowned.

This wasn't going the way Jake had hoped. "This is a shock, right? Take some time to get used to the idea."

She shook her head and handed him the brochure. "I really can't, Jake. I appreciate it a lot and all, but I want to go to Santa Barbara with my friends. I'll live at home the first couple of years."

"Live at home? Has the Admiral been breathing down your neck?" Did the man have no restraint?

"Chill, Jake. I like it at home. Dad's mellowed and I like spending time with Mom."

"But you wanted to go to Europe."

She shrugged. "It was just an idea. And maybe I'll go one day. Just not right out of high school."

It had never occurred to him that she'd react this way. "You can't let them set limits on you. You can do anything you want, be whatever you want, travel the world."

"I know that, Jake," she said softly, leaning toward him. "Listen, I'm not you. Maybe you want to go to Europe—so go. Stop worrying about me. And, while we're on the subject, give Mom and Dad a chance, too. They're different now.

"They've changed. So have you, though you don't seem to notice. You act like you still have to sneak out at night or something."

He took a long drink of strawberry-flavored triple rum. Was she right? Had he locked Penny, his parents, himself into some kind of time capsule? Like that picture on his bureau. He looked at the brochure. Penny had no interest in going to Europe. "I don't get it."

"Exactly," Penny said. "Let me explain it to you."

So she told him about his parents and her, and about high school and the kids she knew and her plans to work at the mall next year, and how the Admiral was giving her his prized Mustang when school started.

The more she talked, the more he realized he'd been blind about a lot of things. There was probably some psychological mumbo-jumbo explanation for it, but he didn't need a therapist to tell him he'd deluded himself.

Penny stayed for another daiquiri before she left to hang with her friends, but not until she'd extracted a promise that he'd come for Sunday dinner at the folks' house. *Really listen to Dad, Jake. He's not the enemy.*

After she left, he took a long swim. A very long swim. And he thought about himself and what he was doing with his life. Was he acting like he was still sixteen and desperate to prove his dad wrong? Did he want more? Like Ariel said? A real job? It was true that sometimes the reasons to avoid a job seemed pointless these days. And seeing Ariel so purposeful and proud of her business had made him think he might be missing something....

He sure as hell didn't want to own any scuba shop, but he had thought about giving lessons on a regular basis—when he wanted and how he wanted—without depending on Brice. Nothing would stop him from starting a school, or hooking up with a scuba shop to offer lessons.

He kept thinking over the next two days as he finished painting the outside of the beach house...and while he refinished the wood floors...and while he bought a couple of pieces of furniture, some house plants, a painting and arranged a deal with his construction buds for adding to the sunporch...

...and when he went to Sunday dinner at his folks and really listened to his father. He went out back to help the Admiral with the pool pump. "Your sister told me what you tried to do," his dad said gruffly, not looking up from the gasket he was scraping. "You go on and live your life your own way. That's what your mother wants for you." Then he cleared his throat, looked up and said softly. "It's what I want for you, too."

Jake nearly hugged him. He still felt his father's disappointment—ten years of it—but for the first time, he felt his love, too.

And Jake started talking. About his life, about teaching diving, maybe starting a school or teaching college classes. They stood out there by the pump until Jake's mother yelled at the Admiral to put the steaks on the grill.

Penny sat there during dinner with a smug look on her face. He hated when she was right.

And somewhere in there, maybe doing the dishes while his mother teased his father about giving up his Mustang, or during the poker game they all played after, he realized that he wanted to spend his life with Ariel.

As much of a pain in the ass as she was, as uptight, over-wrought, jittery and driven as she was, she lit up his life, turned on all the circuits.

He had to let her be who she was—just like he had to let Penny and the Admiral be who they were...and love them anyway. Ariel would be good for him. She'd help him see a little farther than beyond the next wave, which wasn't a bad thing. And he would help her, too, though he'd never change her. He was good for her, too. And now he had to prove it.

EVEN AFTER SHE'D practiced her remarks to perfection, refined her addendum to its most incisive, Ariel had three hours to kill before her appointment with Myron Becker. The Empire State Building was just around the block from her hotel, so she decided to check it out, even though she was probably too nervous to enjoy much.

Ariel made her way through the crowd to the rail at the highest level and looked out over the most amazing city in the world. America's pulse, with all its ambition and passion, desperation and hope, brilliance and beauty—all of it streaming up and down the streets—the veins and arteries of its energetic life.

She heard urgent talking to her left and looked at a woman about her age turned away from the view talking into a cell phone, her other hand covering her far ear. Ariel heard snatches of conversation—*sales figures... inventory...IPO.*

A man wearing a Chicago Bulls baseball cap approached the woman and tugged her arm. "Come on, Jess. You promised this trip you wouldn't."

The woman smiled at him, held up a finger—*just one minute*—then turned back to rattle on with her caller.

With a heavy sigh, the man returned to a telescopic viewer, put money in, and looked out on the city. This kind of thing had happened before to the man, Ariel could tell. She felt sorry for the woman, torn between her work and the man in her life. It was a shame when what people wanted kept them apart.

Ariel took in as much of the place as she could, slowly circling the observation deck three times. So amazing. She kept wishing Jake were here to share it with her. She pushed away the thought—she had no room for self-pity when she had a career to salvage—and managed to get to AutoWerks twenty minutes early.

Finally, she was ushered into Myron Becker's office. He started the meeting with a pointed look at his watch and a chill in his voice, but her energy and ideas gradually thawed him out. When she concentrated, Ariel could accomplish anything, she realized. As long as she stayed focused, didn't get distracted by love or insecurity.

Now, nothing remained but the close. She took a deep breath and began. "So, Myron, as you can see I am prepared to..." *Sacrifice my entire life to work.* Where had that come from? "I'm ready to commit..." *All my joy, all my satisfaction, all my self-worth to making you happy.* Suddenly, she flashed on the picture of the woman at the top of the Empire State Building, who'd had all of Manhattan at her feet, the man she loved calling to her, and she'd remained with the cell phone glued to her ear.

Is that what Ariel wanted? She pictured Jake tugging her out to the sunporch to work in the ocean breeze, taking her for a moonlight swim and scuba diving. That had been important. Good for her. Jake had been good for her. Just the way he was.

"Yes?" Myron looked at her kindly. "You were saying? You're ready to commit...?"

"A reasonable amount of time to your business," she finished in a rush. "I work hard, Myron, and it was wrong of me to leave you hanging. But Business Advantage is not my life. If you're not comfortable with that, then maybe you were right to end our relationship."

He looked at her, shook his head sadly. "You sound like the corporate climate guru we had in here a couple years back. Frequent breaks, generous vacations. Hell, he had us forming a corporate softball team."

"Maybe he had a point."

"I appreciate your honesty," he said, but he sounded annoyed. "I'll have to think about this. Let me get back to you. How long will you be in town?"

"Unless you retain me, I'll leave tomorrow morning," she said. She knew what she wanted now—a life that had time for sand castles and moonlight swims. A life with Jake.

She thought of what her mother had said about her father's fun-loving nature. Maybe he hadn't bought insurance, but he'd put joy in her mother's life. He'd been good for her. Jake had been wrong to dismiss her work, but not wrong to help her enjoy life. She could be like both her parents—fun-loving like her father and sensible like her mother. The point was to stay balanced.

Thinking of her mother, Ariel decided to talk to her about all this, to remind her how important it was to have fun. At the same time, she realized her mother was happy with her life—the diner was her family—and she loved being there.

When she reached her room, she found that Myron had already left a message. "I expect a hundred and ten percent from my employees, but that's probably too much to expect from a consultant. If the managers like your proposal tomorrow, we'll use you for the strategic plan. After that, we'll see."

Ariel had won. Triumph filled her, but she held something back. She knew that even if the managers didn't like her work, she'd be okay. There would be other work. She would manage. She would keep on keeping on.

Part of her was sorry she had to stay through the week. She wanted to talk to Jake, to work things out with him. She called Brice's place, where Jake was staying, and left him the message that she would be back in five days and wanted to talk. She could only hope he wanted to listen.

THE SUPERSHUTTLE VAN left Ariel off on the street above the stairs to the beach house. The strategic plan was a go at AutoWerks, though she'd had to accept a flat fee and no retainer.

She knew she was on her own for sure. She'd called Trudy and learned she and Paul were settling back in London for a while and Trudy had arranged to consult with the new management at the Foster Corporation. *Love takes time and work,* she'd told Ariel. *I didn't build my business overnight. I can't expect any more of my marriage.* And, yes, they planned to tie the knot one day. Ariel was so happy for her. And Trudy had had a good laugh about Ariel falling in love with the easygoing handyman.

Now Ariel stood at the top of the stairs in her suit— the same suit she'd worn when she first arrived—again staring out at the beach, but this time with joy.

The breeze was soft and the air had a salty tang. Why had she thought the beach smelled of seaweed and dead fish? The sun glinted a glorious silver on the waves and she ached to run straight into the water. She recognized Rickie in his green baseball cap playing Frisbee with Lucky on the beach. Somebody's sand castle had begun to crumble. Two bikini-clad models were playing some kind of paddle game to show off their jiggles for muscle-bound dates.

She ran down the stairs, tugged off her shoes, then ducked into the dark hollow under the stairs to slip off her panty hose. She emerged, hefted her bag and set off running.

She loved the ticklish grind and shift of sand under her feet, delighted in the sun on her shoulders. She couldn't wait to see the man she loved. As she got closer, she saw a stack of boards, large plastic buckets and sawhorses beside the house. Jake was still working on the place?

Lord, how would she put up with his distractibility? She bit her lip. The same way he would put up with her compulsive organizing. They would compromise. They loved each other. And love was compromise.

Was this the right thing to do? She thought about her dream husband with his solid job and deep understanding of her ambition. And the house in Thousand Oaks and the golden retriever. She closed her eyes and pictured the scene. Except it seemed more like a Hollywood set than any life she could fit into. Then she pictured Jake in his trunks, with sand in his hair, a surfboard under his arm, dripping saltwater and sand in her kitchen forever and ever, and she smiled. Yeah.

From the porch she caught the blare of rock music. She left her suitcase on the stairs and stepped inside to an amazing sight. The place was perfection. The floors gleamed with new stain. Her desk and shelves were gone from the living room, and Jake had added a gorgeous wallpaper border high on the wall—the one they'd both liked the best, but she couldn't afford. There was a tall ficus tree and an Empress palm, each in a large pot, and a new upholstered armchair. And on the cocktail table was an impossibly beautiful bouquet of tulips.

She stepped forward, stunned, unable even to call Jake's name. The kitchen wore the pin-striped yellow wallpaper she'd chosen and the table held another vase of tulips. She leaned to touch a red flower's cool, waxy surface. Gorgeous.

The door to the sunporch opened and Jake stepped inside. "Ariel," he said, his eyes lit with love.

"You finished everything," she said. "And then some."

"Yeah. Come look." He held the door open so she could see the porch. It had been transformed into an incredible office. The floor had been expanded, covered in a gleaming flagstone and closed in with Plexiglas, giving a breathtaking ocean view. There was even room for a small sofa and cocktail table.

"It makes a great office, don't you think?" Jake said. "It's better for you here than in the city," he said.

"Though I put your desk at an angle, so you can turn away when you feel too distracted."

"How could I turn away from this?" she said, indicating the rolling gray water and the white beach that seemed part of the room. Tears blurred her vision. "It's a million-dollar view...."

"Oh, don't worry about the cost. My friends cut me a deal on the foundation—I bartered some scuba lessons and, since Penny didn't want the Europe trip, I had cash to burn."

Her eyes flew to his. "You shouldn't have spent your money on me."

"Who else would I spend it on? I love you, Ariel."

"Jake," she said, stepping farther into the room, closer to him. She saw that more tulips rested on her desk. "And all the tulips..." Her voice shook.

He shrugged. "They remind me of you."

She loved tulips. Way more than roses. How could she forget? She loved how perfectly they curved—strong, but fragile, too, and rare. And they reminded Jake of her.

She remembered her Mr. Wonderful checklist.... *He'll know me better than I know myself.* Jake had built her the office she needed, not the one she wanted. *He'll bring me roses...* And he'd brought her even better flowers.

"They're perfect," she said. "And so are you."

"I'm not perfect. Far from it. And I'll never have a traditional job. I'm thinking of a scuba school, but who knows. Can you live with that?"

"Absolutely. I will not turn into that woman on the Empire State Building with her ear glued to her phone, her back to the world."

"What?"

"Never mind. Just help me have fun, okay? Until I get the hang of it?"

"For as long as it takes," he said, pulling her into his arms. He kissed her, his lips salty from the sea and warm and full of all the love she knew she'd ever need.

"I hope it takes forever." Beyond Jake's shoulders she could see the beach and the ocean. She thought about those philosophers' metaphors...the endless sand...the ebb and flow, the rhythm of the waves, smoothing the hard edge of everything.

This was not the right time to fall in love, but Jake was right. You can't time love. Or plan it. You just fall into it and make it work.

The only plan she had now was to love Jake, to do her best from day to day. From now on, instead of planning her dream, she'd be living it.

She hated when Jake was right. Except this once.

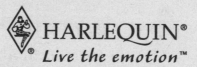

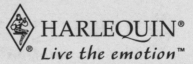

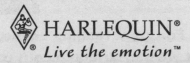

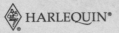

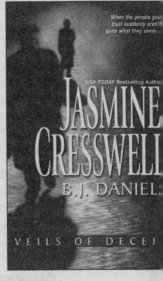

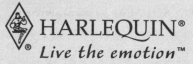
HTH

COMING NEXT MONTH

#949 IT'S ALL ABOUT EVE Tracy Kelleher

When tap pants go missing not once, but *three* times, lingerie-store owner Eve Cantoro calls in the cops. As soon as Carter Moran arrives, he hopes Eve will keep calling, and often! The chemistry between them is red-hot, and as events heat up at the shop, Eve's stock isn't the only lingerie that goes missing....

#950 UNDER FIRE Jamie Denton
Some Like It Hot, Bk. 3

OSHA investigator Jana Linney has never had really *good* sex. So when she meets sexy firefighter Ben Perry, she decides to do something about it. Having a one-night stand isn't like her, but if anyone can "help" her, Ben can. Only, one night isn't enough... and a repeat performance is unlikely, once Jana discovers she's investigating the death of one of Ben's co-workers. Still, now that Jana's tasted what sex *should* be, she's *not* giving it up....

#951 ONE NAUGHTY NIGHT Joanne Rock
The Wrong Bed—linked to Single in South Beach

Renzo Cesare has always been protective toward women. So it makes complete sense for him to "save" the beautiful but obviously out of her league Esmerelda Giles at a local nightclub. But it doesn't make sense for him to claim to be her blind date. He's not sure where *that* impulse came from. But before he can figure out a way to tell her the truth, she's got him in a lip lock so hot, he'll say anything to stay there!

#952 BARELY BEHAVING Jennifer LaBrecque
Heat

After three dead-end trips down the matrimonial highway, Tammy Cooper is giving up on marriage. She's the town bad girl—and she's proud of it. From now on, her motto is "Love 'em and leave 'em." Only, her plan takes a hit when gorgeous veterinarian Niall Fortson moves in next door. He's more than willing to let Tammy love him all she wants. But he's not letting her go anywhere....